Cabbages in the Air

By

Carol-Ann Errington

Grosvenor House
Publishing Limited

This book is published by
Grosvenor House Publishing Ltd
Link House
140 The Broadway, Tolworth, Surrey, KT6 7HT.
www.grosvenorhousepublishing.co.uk

This book is a work of fiction. Any resemblance to
people or events, past or present, is purely coincidental.

A CIP record for this book
is available from the British Library

ISBN 978-1-83615-243-9

Following a career in teaching, Carol-Ann began a MA degree in Creative Writing. It was at this time that she fell in love with the short story; its form immediately appealed to her. And although small, unlike its dominant relative, the novel, it can be ambitious, engaging and memorable.

Cabbages in the Air

A pale hand jerked upwards to shield his eyes as Stanley Horner searched the early evening sky for his beloved pigeons. Pigeons, all eighteen of them, to you and I would probably look pretty much the same. But not to Stanley. He named every one of them, from Ricky Rickster to Gilbert the Great. He could recognise them instantly and without hesitation by their greyness—from ghostly pale to battleship dark. Or by the beadiness of an eye and quirkiness of gait, and most definitely by the shimmering mauve of Hettie and Agnes. To say they were his sole interest in life doesn't quite paint the picture. They were the love of his life—a passion unequalled, unrivalled.

And then there was his wife, Joan. Gentle Joan, who for almost forty years had played second fiddle to the likes of Hettie and Agnes. She was a doggedly selfless woman who had served her husband's dinner at precisely 5.30pm every day of her married life and made him countless cups of sweetened, brown tea on command. She had listened to his constant mutterings about sacks of grain or the general health of Ricky or Gilbert. Joan, who was rarely able to have an actual conversation with Stan. Nobody could. There was no exchanging of views or ideas, nothing remotely interactive about his method of communication. He made pigeon related statements. He did not expect or require a response.

Poor Joan.

Gentle Joan. Nobody knew Joan; Joan knew nobody—except her Stan of course. Every day she would pick up her straw shopping bag, secure her light brown head-scarf over her white curls with a simple knot under the chin, slip into her faded but spotlessly clean beige raincoat and walk down the road in the direction of the butcher and grocer. Just occasionally a neighbour might catch sight of her and wish her good morning, to which she would reply in her soft voice, 'Ah, good morning.' Then she would be gone, striding towards her destination. A bit of stewing beef or a string of sausages from Mr Boyce, then on to Miss White for a few apples or boiling potatoes. Miss White's store sold just about everything, which is fine if you didn't mind outdated tins, dusty shelves or packets so old that the colour had faded and labelling had ceased to exist. Shopping done, Joan would retrace her steps home to number one-nine-seven, along the same pavements she had known for seven decades. Her short figure, round shouldered of late, moved with care and precision, cocooned against a world she found increasingly alien and unpredictable.

As a matter of fact Joan loved animals. All animals, great and small. She would have loved a small pet—a little dog or cat maybe. But Stan was dead against such a thing, a fact that was becoming too unreasonable for her to bear. He would stubbornly oppose any suggestion, 'It's bad enough with that bloody black cat next door. It sits there Joan, eyeing my beauties. I swear I'll kill it if it catches my Hattie or Agnes.'

Joan knew better these days. She never mentioned the subject again.

Over the years, Stan had invented several ways to guide his birds home. A firm favourite of his was to shake a red biscuit tin full of seeds whilst hollering 'Come on. Come on.' Apparently his familiar voice accompanied by the percussive sound did the trick. But on most evenings, post liver and onions or toad-in-the-hole, the little man would stand in his back garden, shirt sleeves rolled and trousers hoisted to chest level, preparing for action. Under each arm he held an ageing Savoy cabbage, which from time to time he would hurl in the air to guide his beloved ones home. Cabbages were never actually eaten, they were grown specifically for this essential duty.

When dusk arrived and his beauties were home, safe and chattering contentedly in their loft, Stan would settle himself in his rattan chair in the shelter of the lean-to. From here he could keep watch, as a shepherd might his sheep, until the sky turned inky black. Joan sat in her little front room darning his socks.

13th September arrived, the day of their annual trip to Bury St Edmunds. A tiny flutter of excitement grew in Joan's belly as she bustled in the kitchen, preparing potted meat sandwiches and a flask of strong brown tea. She eyed the clock, removed her apron that covered her best pleated skirt and called to her husband, 'Are you ready, Stan? We must be on our way now.'

'Can't go yet, Joan. The grain's not been delivered.'

At midday, Joan was still waiting. Two hours later she rose from her chair, climbed the narrow staircase to her room and changed into her everyday clothes.

The neatly pressed pleated skirt was returned to her wardrobe. She brushed away a silent tear as it rolled down her cheek.

Stan was delighted when, at 4pm, the grain was delivered. Had he noticed, he probably wouldn't have been able to interpret the disappointment etched on his wife's face.

On the morning of 14th September Joan stood at her bedroom window and there was Stan strutting up and down the garden path, his bald head glowing in the morning sun. And then Joan felt a swelling, as if her whole body was suddenly filled with the slow creep of resentment. A resentment that she had not allowed to take hold; after all it was her duty to quell her desires and expectations, wasn't it? Well she was a fool. Her hands felt for her belly that had never held a child. 'No, we're fine Joan. Just the two of us.' That's what he always said. Her hands dropped to her side and floundered a little in the folds of her skirt. 'Oh well, too late...' she whispered as she moved away from the window, swept a stray silver curl back into place and made her way downstairs to the kitchen. She eyed the kitchen clock: Stan would be in for lunch in an hour. She remembered the chicken stock from yesterday— that would do. She would add some root vegetables and make a nice broth. As she rolled back the sleeves of her daisy-print blouse, her hand briefly circled her wrist, where a bruise had turned brown. She sliced and diced the vegetables and hardly flinched when the knife cut into her flesh and released a crimson trickle of her life. Precious life. It wasn't too late.

Joan found an old suitcase under the stairs. It smelt a little musty, its locks were quite rusty and it hadn't been used for many years, but it would do. Unrushed, she began to fill it with a few essential belongings, and in the layers she placed her Building Society book. She had squirrelled away a little money every year of her married life, and now her thrift would be repaid. She picked up her framed wedding photo taken in August 1945. There was Stan with his head held high, just inching above hers and his shoes had been polished until they shone. But no. She replaced the photo. It belonged to Stan now. She closed the suitcase and placed a small white envelope marked 'Stanley' on the little table in the hall, then walked to the front door where she paused momentarily before closing it behind her for the very last time.

It was the bravest thing she had ever done.

Two days later Stan was found by a couple of pigeon fanciers who had come for a bit of advice. He lay on the path in his back garden. His lifeless body surrounded by his beloved birds who cooed and pecked in an attempt to resuscitate him.

'Bloody hell! Must have been a heart attack. Where's Joan?'

The Silence

The tiny hairs on the back of his neck sprang up as a cautionary wind blew down the street. But, thought Rob, this is moving-in day; everything is bound to feel — well—strange ... Isn't it?

Feeling completely drained and nearing a state of inertia, Rob called a break and headed into the kitchen where he rummaged in the large cardboard box to find the kettle, mugs, milk and tea-bags. As he waited for the water to boil, his brow furrowed as he noticed minor but in-need-of-repair faults in several parts of the room. There was a bloody three to four millimetre gap between the left side of the window frame and the wall; this was an absolute dream world for draughts and various members of the insect population and must be fixed tomorrow. An overhead cupboard door fell open at his touch and swung, elbow-like, on one hinge before crashing down onto the work-surface, then the floor, as it relieved itself of its burden, but in doing so inflicted a painful blow onto Rob's big toe.

'Okay okay, Rob, let's call it a day,' said Essie as she rushed into the kitchen, 'we're both knackered. I'll go find the arnica gel for that toe, and I think we should pop round to our new neighbours and introduce ourselves – as you do.'

'What? Oh yeah ... right, fine.'

Both wearing smiles – hers genuine – his contrived, the young couple approached the first house to the right. Unlike theirs, this house was large, bulky and quite brutish in stature; its bold prominent window headers drooped like heavy eyelids; its cast iron gate growled reluctantly as it was pushed open. As Rob's eyes flicked over the frontage, he glimpsed a face half hidden behind a black, twitching curtain, but the two knocked and chatted as they waited to be welcomed into the village community. No one came. Undeterred, they tried the house to the left: an unmoving figure at an upstairs window watched as the smiles slipped away from the newcomers. As before, no one stirred to answer the door. They tried further down the High Street in which they now lived.

But no one came. No one answered.

A seed of anxiety now took hold: Rob's thoughts were now mingled with unease, but Essie offered an explanation, 'It's fine. They must like to keep to themselves; we can handle that.'

Rob turned away as he uttered a mild response, as if to protect her from the negative thoughts etched on his face.

But the next few weeks were filled with the business of settling in. Essie's enthusiasm was infectious and helped quell Rob's anxieties. He thought she looked particularly happy when she arrived home from work, one evening.

'Hey, Rob.'

'Hey, you.'

'D'you fancy a few drinks at the pub tonight? They do meals too.'

He smiled at her lightheartedness and reached for her hand, 'Great idea. We should check out the local, and with a bit of luck we might actually find a friendly face.'

The Rising Sun, a charming 17th century hostelry, lay at the far end of the High Street: its garden to the rear rolled down to meet a lazy stream that bumbled unhurriedly by. Rob and Essie strolled past the village school a fairly unremarkable single storey Victorian building, except for one remarkable fact: there were no children in the village. 'Don't you think that's weird, Ess. Have you actually seen a child since we moved in?'

'Well no, I haven't. Must be some explanation – maybe we'll...'

But as they pushed open the heavy oak door and entered the bar, the warm chatter ceased, and they were met by a dozen hostile faces who quickly manoeuvred themselves to fill all the available seats. Rob's head began to prickle, but undeterred he waited to be served, although there was no queue, no visible reason why he should have to wait, other than the landlord turning his back to him as he shifted bottles unnecessarily from left to right and back again.

Lifting his voice, Rob called, 'Two large glasses of house red, please.' Gathering thoughts urged him to leave as Essie's hand grabbed his elbow, but no, he stood firm, he had made a request. The clock ticked loudly as he felt their stares penetrate his body. When the drinks eventually appeared in front of him, he offered a note in payment and held out his hand to receive the change; but the outstretched hand remained empty and foolish as the coins were slapped noisily onto the counter in front of him.

Not wishing to stand on a lonely stage, they headed for the garden, not caring that the autumnal wind blew and their jackets were thin. They had little to say to each other; he looked to the east, she looked to the west. The evening's promise cruelly crushed, Rob fought against the blame game. But the seed of doubt was planted. They walked home in silence. The gap between them, whilst not deliberate, and barely measurable, was most definitely there.

The next morning Rob decided to check out the school; a little nosy around might reveal one or two answers to the mounting questions. A short walk along the High Street and he was there, standing outside the gates which were locked and chained; but where there was a dip in the railings he managed to leap over and land in the abandoned playground. He stood and listened. He listened and was certain that he could hear the faint shadowy echoes of children's voices. Peering through grimy windows, he could make out the sad emptiness of two classrooms. Tiny tables and chairs; paint pots; a globe and pegs for little coats. There were no children, of course.

As he leapt back onto the pavement, an elderly cyclist slowed and wobbled to a halt.

'You won't find any children there you know. Been closed for the best part of twenty years now. Funny business.'

'What happened?' said Rob.

'Well… there were no more children.'

'Why?'

'Don't think anyone knows for sure … Something about … Oh I don't know… Miscarriages and things like that. Anyway, it's a rum place and I'm glad I don't live here.'

And then she was gone; her lemon-yellow scarf trailing behind her. Rob tried to call her back, 'Yes but … Hey … Just a minute.'

On the way home he tussled with the idea of keeping this information to himself, although he knew Essie should know. But he did not tell her.

The hostility grew, cancerous in its design, unwavering in its delivery. The short walk to the village shop was now avoided. How many times had Rob entered to the welcoming tinkle of the bell, only to find himself strangely manoeuvred to the back of the queue? Protestations fell on deaf ears.

'Hey, excuse me… I've been here for fifteen minutes…'

'Well now, Mrs Kibbling,' said the narrow shopkeeper, 'you'll be needing to get to your appointment. What was it you wanted? Oh good morning, Baz. What can I get for you? Don't want you being late for work, that would never do.'

Rob's head filled with frustration and a simmering anger that spread to his fists. 'Excuse me. Did you hear what I just said?'

Five heads swivelled. Their eyes steadily draining of colour as they riveted themselves upon Rob. Not a sound passed their lips, but as he watched the heaving chests rise and fall, the small space seemed robbed of oxygen, and he fled outside to compose, to control himself, before reaching home.

Finding the shop empty was no better. He could see in from across the road, but by the time he reached the door, a hand flipped the 'open' sign and a blind was swiftly unfurled. A snub. Not wanted.

Once home, he would hover restlessly by the front window, anxious to tell Essie.

'I never get served. I. Never. Get. Served! What the hell's going on here?'

Essie flung off her coat and held his shoulders, 'It's probably something and nothing. Give them time, they'll come round... Some folks take time, that's all.'

'I'm here all the time, Ess. I don't feel ... There's something—'

'Oh come on, we'll be fine... remember why we moved here, and it's going to be perfect for your writing!'

Doggedly determined to get to grips with his work, and well aware of fast approaching deadlines, Rob rearranged his room so that his desk was facing a blank wall and not the High Street. The wall was palest blue and perfect. No prints. No ditzy patterns. Staring into this soft blueness, he could drift into new worlds: sub worlds; forgotten worlds; delve into creations as yet unknown to him.

Settling down, with fingers flying on the keyboard, they suddenly slowed and slithered to a stop. Rob's brow furrowed, partly because of the interruption but mainly due to a curiosity that swelled into a foreboding. A thrumming sound assaulted his ears and filled his head. He sat perfectly still, eyes blinking as he tried in vain to identify the invasive noise. It was cyclical in design: a round of crescendo and diminuendo, each lasting thirty seconds. He left his desk in search of the source. Maybe a malfunctioning radio? But no. The thrum was constant and tortuous; he longed for the diminuendo but dreaded the crescendo. 'Neighbours! It's got to be! Of all the bloody inconsiderate things ...'

He flew out of the house prepared for a confrontation, but he found nothing at all, nothing but silence. He stood there utterly exasperated and perplexed until a tractor chugged past; its ordinariness, its haplessness, gathered his senses and led him indoors where he stuffed cotton wool in his ears and attempted to continue his work. He failed of course.

He didn't hear Essie arrive home—missed her key in the door.

'Hey you, what's with the stuffed ears?'

Rob's fingers snatched away the bungs. 'Oh hi ... Wait, it's stopped! There's been a constant thrumming noise here all day!'

'Are you sure? Coming from where? Probably from one of your crazy, mind-of- their-own radios you refuse to get rid of.'

'No, I checked, even went outside. Thought it could be the neighbours.'

'Oh, well that's really odd,' said Essie, as she linked arms with Rob and led him into the kitchen, 'Maybe it's that imagination of yours again! Come on, let's eat and I'll tell you all about Little-Miss-Bloody-Tedium at work.'

Rob wasn't listening. He could see her mouth moving, her head bobbing, but the thrumming of the day lingered and jarred, refusing to make way for a morsel of peace.

The following day, there it was again, the second after Essie left for work. The most unwelcome sound he could imagine, THRUM. Rob drove to Burford, the nearest town, and after locating an industrial 'outfitters', he purchased a robust looking pair of defenders. Eyeing Rob's fine woollen, v-necked sweater and unblemished chinos, the shop assistant felt the urge to query the purchase. 'You in the construction business then? Only you don't look like—' Rob interrupted him, 'Yeah, well, I'm thinking of maybe changing … It's those pneumatic drills …'

'Oh I see,' came the response from the perplexed looking assistant. 'Right, you'll be needing them then.'

All the way home Rob was thrilled at the idea of beating the bastards – whoever, whatever they are.'

Settling down at his desk, confident that no sound could penetrate the defenders, he stared at his blue wall and prepared himself for the familiar journey into other worldliness. He was right on one count: he heard nothing. Silence. But as his fingers dared to move around the keyboard, they paused, his head drooped and he slumped forward as he felt vibrations: vivid, powerful, surging through his body like waves pulsating and pounding the seashore. Snatching off the defenders, he left the house and ran blindly until he could run no more, and all his visceral anger had dissipated. What remained was a very deep sadness, born of regret and frustration. Why? Why him? What had he done? He sank down onto a grassy bank and marvelled at its bold greenness, its simplicity, its normality. Rob knew that there was nothing 'normal' about his life now. He wished he'd never set eyes on the godforsaken place but Essie was so keen, he just had to agree. But hadn't he known? Didn't he sense something vaguely sinister at first sight? An uncommon stillness? Irrational or what? Paranoia had set in. He knew that; hadn't Essie thought so too? He caught her side-long looks, those unfinished sentences. So unlike her.

'Why have you …'

'Do you think you should …'

'Whenever I come home …'

His watch told him that Essie would soon be home and so he stood up, sighed deeply, and walked home to the house that he wished didn't belong to him. But hey! He would not share his fears with her this evening. Let her believe he'd had a good day.

Throughout the evening he chatted companionably, which brought a smile to her lips and that 'almost there' glitter to her eyes. As she moved to draw the curtains, he watched her pause, mid-sentence, as her hand held the edge.

'How strange! Have you seen this, Rob? There are three people standing on the pavement outside our house, and they're staring right in!'

He was at her side instantly. He looked. He saw. Standing shoulder to shoulder were two men and a woman all wearing calf-length, brown shapeless coats. They stood still; only a small breeze ruffled the woman's hair. Hastily closed curtains removed the unwanted faces.

They returned the next evening, and the next . Rob was livid, 'Enough! The police need to know about this!' So he called, he explained, and he demanded action.

'Yes, but Mr … what was the name?'

'It's Mitchum.'

'Right Mr Mitchum, I understand your concern, but you say these people aren't actually doing anything. Have they harmed you in any way?'

'No but … Then there's the noise … Every day … I can't work.'

'Noise, sir? Is it coming from the neighbours?'

'No, but …'

'I tell you what, just to put your mind at rest, I'll send a patrol car to have a little look as soon as I can. Goodbye Mr Mitchum.'

'They don't believe me. Think I'm some sort of crank!' said Rob.

'I agree it's all a bit weird and unsettling,' said Essie, 'but those people haven't actually committed an offence.'

'Yet!' said Rob.

Just then his phone throbbed into action; his eyes narrowed, he breathed heavily as he read the text: 'Now why go and do a silly thing like that! Calling the police – naughty! Mustn't do that again.'

'Who the hell is this! How does anybody know I've just called the police?'

'Calm down Rob, please! They'll get bored, then they'll leave us alone. You'll see.'

He knew she was wrong; he was getting a little bit fed up with her 'It'll be fine' approach to everything, because it bloody well wasn't. He felt his heart hammering higher, up into his throat; his shoulders locked and his breath felt heavier than he'd ever known.

Each day he would count one more villager clad in brown standing shoulder to shoulder, heads fixed and eyes riveted. They made no sound. Rob raged at them from his doorstep, 'Why are you here? What do you want with us? Leave us ALONE! LEAVE US ALONE! He marched to the pavement and raged in their faces, but they stood unflinching and motionless. The villagers of Holyfeld would not leave them alone.

One evening the antagonists no longer stood on the pavement, but one by one with slow determination they filled the newcomers' front garden, booted feet thumping the ground, and with a synchronised grinding of heels they crushed the life out of every stem of the beautiful French lavender; the fragrant sea of purple.

Now the pack was ready for the hunt. Shoulder to shoulder they moved instinctively down the sides of the house to the rear, where they filled every window with their ghoulish faces; their colourless eyes. Contorted tongues, noses and foreheads, splattered and smeared the panes. No word was spoken, but as Rob and Essie looked up, sensing a sudden darkness, the pack moved in for the kill. Mouths opened, stretched wide, as the words GO AWAY! were repeated soundlessly and in unison. The horrified newcomers stood petrified, unable to move, until Essie, hands clutching her head, let out a piercing scream that delighted the gyrating mob into a silent frenzy. At this, Rob leapt forward, snatching at the curtains, shutting out the nightmare. The gruesome faces with the colourless eyes now retreated, confident that their work was done. They had their prey.

By the middle of the night the newcomers had fled, their car filled with hastily packed suitcases and cardboard boxes. So swift was their exit that the next morning it was noted that a man's black shoe and a framed photograph of the smiling couple had been left behind – dropped, it was thought, as they ran down the garden path. Now these innocent items awaited their own fate.

A collective sigh of contentment could be heard rising above the village of Holyfeld. Cheerful voices greeted each other as they went about their daily business. Waving hands met with broad smiles as friends and neighbours cycled by. Endless random acts of kindness soothed troubles and smoothed furrowed brows. So joyful were they in their collectiveness.

They were good people, weren't they?

Until the next time.

Last Supper

A tired plastic clock on the tiled wall of a fish and chip shop summons Ernie Waterhouse to begin the day's work. It is 10.30am. Ernie, all knobs and bones, shuffles in: his corns are killing him and his unwashed hair sticks thinly to his scalp.

Ernie's father, Albert, had opened the establishment in Chuffingham back in 1949, when folks on Waxworth Street were proud to see such an 'enterprising venture' in their own backyard. Under the stewardship of Mr Waterhouse snr., the business thrived. His fish was always cooked to perfection: using a simple flour and water batter, he would add a little baking soda and a touch of vinegar to create a light and bubbly batter—best in the county, some were heard to say. And his chips, presented in a cone made from yesterday's newspaper, were a rare treat; just add a sprinkling of salt and a dash of vinegar and they were yours to savour. Nowadays, it was a case of bust rather than boom.

The more discerning fish and chip lovers might well suggest that it is the quality of the food on sale rather than a general decline in the popularity of the nation's national dish. And then of course there are the premises. *Food and Hygiene Standards* would have a field day! They'd be rubbing their hands in glee. 'Whoa... What have we here? When was this place last inspected?' Run a finger along the walls to find rancid grease; grease that has been allowed to build and flourish, lying undisturbed for years. Definitely not the high gloss finish of a tiled wall that you thought it was. Nevertheless, Ernie and his wife, Ethel, were largely oblivious to their unhealthy working conditions and cared even less about the comfort of their customers and the mucky surfaces awaiting the unsuspecting fish and elderly potatoes.

Still, it is Monday morning and there's money to be made—albeit a modest amount these days. Ethel puffs in behind her husband: she breathes uneasily on account of her expanding girth and the numerous cigarettes that have violated her once admired form. Husband and wife exchange a series of grunts—incoherent mumblings to the onlooker, but listlessly acceptable to the Waterhouses. Ethel's newly bleached red hair is covered by an off-white cap, set at a rakish angle and decorated with a row of grimy fingermarks. She wears a canary-yellow nylon apron and her sleeves are rolled up in a haphazard fashion to reveal huge forearms that loll, seal-like, on the counter.

Ernie slowly cranks himself into action: the murky frying fat begins to heat whilst he sends each potato to be sliced and shaped into the groaning chipper—thunk and slam, thunk and slam. Ethel's forearms continue to loll on the counter; her generous behind is wedged against the fryer whilst pale eyes roll lazily towards the clock. 'It's comin' up 11. I'll go get them pies and put a bit of glaze on them, and they'll never know how old they are. Serves the buggers right… That'll teach them. How dare they complain… She disappears into the back of the shop licking her spiteful lips.

Meanwhile, Ernie dumps grey-fleshed fish unceremoniously into thick, sticky batter, then plunges them into the awaiting cauldron of bubbling, stale fat. What a fate.

It is 11.30am. Ethel huffs and puffs her way to the door where she flicks over the 'closed' sign and splats her nose and cheeks against the glass panel—an alarming sight to anyone who has the misfortune to be passing by. She cares not a jot as her eyes rove up and down the windswept street where litter is tossed high into the air then plunges and clings onto lamp posts or becomes ensnared in a balding hedge. At 12.05 old Mickey Mulch from number 109 jerks open the door and sidles in.

'Cod and a large bag of chips. An' I hope that there fish is better than Wednesday's was. Me belly gave me hell all bloody night.'

'Nowt to do with *my* fish,' Ernie snaps back. 'Fresh every day. Fresh every day.'

Ethel sneezes as she bundles chips into a well-used sheet of newspaper: thousands of hapless microbes are dispatched every which way. Most, of course, make an invisible landing on Mickey's lunch.

The old clock struggles on as it ekes out its last bit of energy. A handful of hungry customers drop by as the afternoon is slowly eaten away. They moan about the miserly portions and threaten not to buy anymore, to which Ernie's lip reacts with a curl. A small group of teen-aged girls and boys burst in after school, their dark uniforms heavily compromised, their ties askew. Ethel longs to stuff their loud mouths with last year's pickled eggs—it's a recurrent dream of hers. And then they're gone; they spill out onto the street, filling the air with shrieks and raucous renditions.

At 5.30pm the Waterhouses prepare for the early evening 'rush'. Ernie shouts from the back of the shop. 'Ready for the grand finale, Ethel? I reckon a special Waterhouse batter is in order tonight. A very special one.'

'A *very* special one,' replies Ethel. She empties the usual ingredients into the batter bowl; the large rusty blades rotate and blend, rotate and blend. But now there's a treat in store for this evening's punters: she reaches down beneath the counter and lifts a sack containing the finest quality golden saw-dust and watches keenly as it falls silently into the batter. The obedient blades rotate and blend, rotate and blend. This evening Ernie's grin is huge and long lasting. So is his wife's.

By 8.0pm they've sold twelve cod and chips and six-super sized sausages (in extra thick batter). Ernie moves to flick over the 'open' sign, then husband and wife make their way up the stairs to their living quarters: this is an arduous task for the Waterhouses—the ascent is slow and there is a great deal of huffing and puffing. The stairs groan in sympathy or suffering. Having recovered their breath, they rip away their mucky aprons and grab their ready-packed suitcases. The old plastic clock stumbles at 8.15pm. Then it stops.

They do not lock the back door as they leave. Why bother? They pile their luggage into the boot of their brown, slightly rusting Ford Zephyr and speed away without a backward glance. Not one final glance at the home and workplace they had shared for thirty years.

As a consequence of eating their evening meal, eighteen people are taken ill that evening: some are rushed to Chuffingham General while others suffer a digestive nightmare. Nobody is around when the *Food and Hygiene Standards* people come to inspect the local chippy, or when the police call to ask some questions. The front page of the Chuffingham Chronicle contains angry quotes from the outraged public and the search for the dastardly duo extends into months. But the errant Waterhouses are far away. They are masters of disguise.

Taxi

The journey from Edinburgh seemed endless; passengers' loud voices hammered in her head and Evelyn longed for space, quiet and fresh air. Her feet twitched and in her hands she held, like a talisman, the photograph of her mother. A woman unknown to her. And now the search was over, Evelyn would meet her at last. Not long now.

It was late afternoon and her destination was near at hand as she turned ro view the Fenland region: its great flatness revealing mile upon mile of summer crops ... hardly a tree in sight. Red roofs, bold spires and a host of proud chimneys appeared in the distance. The rhythm of the train relaxed and slowed as Evelyn realised she was approaching March, on the banks of the river Nene. Relieved to escape the sweltering carriage, she grabbed her few belongings, scrambled her way to the opening doors and out onto the platform that was bathed in glittery sunshine.

She shaded her eyes, gulped in fresh air and stood for a few seconds before finding the taxi rank. She was so close now. But then a terrible thought held her fast ... What if her mother wasn't there? Changed her mind ... or... didn't answer the door? What then? Was she prepared for the possibility... No, no, no—unthinkable Dark patches had spread in the armpits of her new linen jacket; she snatched it off, knowing that she looked a mess. Her hair was flat, her dress limp and her face a deepening shade of pink. Tiny beads of sweat began to gather conspiratorially on her forehead; she swiped them away with her hand, took a deep breath and joined the short taxi queue. Twelve miles to Middleton, where her mother lived. So near.

But now the waiting time was over as she settled into the back of the taxi, her destination explained to the driver whose dark blond hair sprang in spikes from her head as if in permanent alarm. Fascinating, thought Evelyn, and she wondered if such a style required lots of tweeking with super strong hair gel. She supposed it did—all that faffing about first thing in the morning.

Again anxiety arose as she thought of her mother who had chosen to live without her. She hadn't minded sharing her life with somebody else's mother had she? That wasn't the point—but why? Why had her mother let go of her at birth ... as if she were tarnished goods? Evelyn had always sensed ... something like a shadow nudging ... questioning ... whispering ... to know—find answers. Ok, enough! She needed to focus on the here and now. What expression should she wear when she came face to face with her mother? A broad smile — suggests openness and warmth, or perhaps a small gentle smile, showing promise. Evelyn chewed at the wart on her forefinger before realising what she was doing and snatched her finger away. If it bleeds it will spread, she reminded herself.

She reached for her small hairbrush and mirror, and attempted to coax her copper coloured hair into some sort of shape. Hopeless. A dash of tangerine lipstick would have to do. As she licked her finger and patted down the unruly eyebrows, it occurred to her that perhaps she had inherited them from her mother—just a thought—hard to tell from the photo. Right. No more rehearsing questions and answers; she was as prepared as she was ever going to be and just about keeping palpitations at bay.

The thick, flat voice of the taxi driver broke the silence. 'Sorry, won't be a sec … desperate for the loo,' as they stopped outside a petrol station and the woman hot-footed round to the rear of the building.

Five minutes slid by before Evelyn realised that she was still waiting for the driver to return. She frowned as she peered out of the windows in all directions. A small white van drove away in the direction of March, but that was it. No one. No vehicles. Another minute went by—she felt a fizz of anger effervesce inside her. She released her seatbelt, stepped out of the taxi, slamming the door and strode across the forecourt in search of the driver. The place looked deserted, passing traffic few and far between. The petrol station backed onto open fields; she walked to the perimeter fence and searched the flat landscape – nothing except a tiny moving dot far away in the distance—a tractor she presumed.

Turning, she entered the toilet block and shivered slightly at the soiled dankness—typical of such places. They appeared empty, but this didn't stop Evelyn from shouting, 'Hello,'as if someone might be hard of hearing or having a nap. Silence. The silence that feels very loud and very long. Panicking now, she nudged open the cubicle door—just in case … She needed to check her driver hadn't collapsed and was slumped on the floor. But no. The creep of anxiety lurked nearby as she retraced her steps and made her way to the front of the building where she entered the Co-op shop.

Empty; but then she caught sight of an assistant, head bowed as he pored over a magazine. 'Excuse me,'asked Evelyn, 'excuse me, but has a middle-aged woman been in here recently?'

'Nah. Must be at least an hour since anyone's been in here. Sorry.'

'Are you sure because …'

'Like I said, no, not in the past hour,' interrupted the assistant as he shifted moodily from his stool, turned his back and began the unnecessary task of tidying shelves. Heart thudding, Evelyn left the shop and headed for the taxi, where she found her phone and prepared to call the taxi rank. She couldn't. There was no signal. She was very conscious of the time – it was now past six o'clock; she had told her mother to expect her before six—if her train was delayed she would let her know. Oh my God! She'll think I've changed my mind.

She sat very still, willing herself to know what to do, her eyes darting as she forced an answer, and at that moment she caught sight of the key—still in the ignition where the driver had left it. So she must have intended to be straight back! But where the hell was she? Her eyes remained riveted on the key as she determined her next move. She guessed she must be about half-way to Middleton—too far to walk either way, but she could just about remember the route from March station. She made one more search for the missing driver, her footsteps echoing, tip tapping as she scanned the whole area, peeping behind the building—just in case. Nothing. She decided to check again in the Co-op. It was empty of customers but the assistant was still poring over a magazine. Evelyn sighed deeply. 'Sorry to bother you again but are you sure you haven't seen a middle-aged woman... Maybe you saw her pass the window on her way to the conveniences—'

'The what? Nah, you're the first woman I've seen all afternoon.'

Evelyn felt sure that he wouldn't notice if the shop or forecourt was filled with women—or men, for that matter—because his magazine was so absorbing. 'I don't suppose there's a landline phone I could use?

'Nah. Sorry mate.'

She returned to the car. Ok, there was no signal so phone calls were out of the question; it was too far to walk either way. She had little choice; she must drive back to the taxi rank where she would explain her predicament, then get to her mother as quickly as possible. Sweaty palms gripped the steering wheel. She paused before manoeuvering the car back onto the road in the direction of March. The roar of necessity quickly overwhelmed silent voices of unease.

There were plenty of road signs, but she didn't need them: her sense of direction was second to none. With the railway station now in view, she slowed as she approached the taxi rank where several drivers stood stretching their legs, drinking coffee and smoking. As soon as she drove over, four drivers moved towards her. 'Where's Madge?' said one of them, his hand rested on the roof of the car as if claiming ownership. Evelyn got out of the car, face flushed, eager to explain her predicament. She explained how the driver had needed a toilet break and how she had waited five or six minutes for her, then when she didn't return she had searched everywhere—even asked in the shop. There was no phone signal so she couldn't phone the taxi rank—that was when she noticed the key still in the ignition... 'Now wait a minute,' said the barrel-chested man, moving closer to her, 'you don't seriously expect us to believe that cock-and-bull story, do you? We know for a fact that Madge would *never* leave the car mid-journey, not even for a minute—it's standard procedure. Where is she?'

Evelyn fought panic. Fought the desire to run. 'I have no idea. I'm sorry I can't be of more help, but if you'll just let me continue my journey ...'

'I'm calling the police,' said another driver as he held up his phone, 'I don't like the sound of this. I think you, young lady, should stay right here.'

She no longer felt the desire to run—it would only make matters worse. Her head drooped, her heart thumped, then sank. She was innocent wasn't she? How could she be responsible for the missing driver? She was on her way to meet her mother for goodness sake! How they'd looked at her—accusing—pointing—narrowing eyes at her ... How could it have happened to her on this of all days? Why her? Her mother wouldn't be there now would she ... Probably not ... Given up on her ...Again.

She listened to the words of the police officer; words that grew distant—wandered away from her. How could they possibly be about her? 'The driver of this taxi is missing. We believe you, Evelyn Thomas, were the last person to see her today. We would like you to accompany us to the police station to help us with our enquiries.' Desperate words tumbled. 'Will you allow me to phone my mother... She...She's expecting—'

'You'll get the opportunity later,' interrupted the officer, 'I'm afraid I'll have to ask you to hand over your mobile phone.' As Evelyn was guided into the back of the police car, her eyes swept the gathering onlookers. She was searching for her mother's face.

They asked many questions. She couldn't help them. She hated the way they probed and insinuated. She was no liar. She couldn't help them — she knew nothing. Questions, questions. She started to weep — she was ashamed of that. 'Yes but Miss Thomas, I think *you* need to think very carefully. You can see how things aren't stacking up for us. You were her last customer— and now she's missing.'

'I told you ... I was on my way to see my mother ... And now ... And now...' Her hands leapt to steady her head. She felt the walls of the interview room closing in on her. Why didn't they believe her? They didn't believe her because she was tarnished goods ... That's what she was. And where was her mother?

Sylvia

It took Sylvia's mother ten years to die. Ten years, three months and six days to be precise. Sylvia could pinpoint the beginning of her mother's demise to November 1980: she just took to her bed and that was that. 'It's my heart Sylvie,' her mother had said, 'you need to look after me now. You can pack that job in straight away and those daft friends of yours. No more gallivanting for you young lady. I've been a good mother to you, so now it's your turn. Can't expect our Angie to do anything, what with that good job of hers. She's a supervisor now you know …' Sylvia stared at the brown stain on the yellow wallpaper just above her mother's head. She couldn't remember how it got there. 'Are you listening to me Sylvie? Brains of the family, is our Angie. And you can forget about courting too. Mind, you're no oil painting—they'll not be queueing up will they?'

Sylvia had spent her childhood endlessly seeking her mother's approval. She always failed. However hard she tried she remained in the shadow of her younger sister, Angie. Sylvia still missed her father—she knew she had been special to him—He'd always had a broad smile for her, or a warm hand on her shoulder to comfort or praise. His death had left her bereft, the pain unbearable. A chill had entered her soul. 'Stop moping around the place Sylvie,' her mother had said as she fixed a new red

31

ribbon in Angie's shiny black hair, 'it won't bring him back. What about me and your sister?'

Sylvia understood her place. She toiled without complaint—what would have been the point anyway? She fetched and carried; she bathed her mother's unsightly feet and massaged her fleshy white legs. Whenever Sylvia had to leave the house, she suspected her mother was up and about: that tell-tale mud on the sides of her slippers, or a sudden shortage of custard creams. But she had learned to say nothing. Mother's cruel tongue made her wince like a sharp pain in her chest. Angie, of course, always promised to 'Pop by next weekend.'She never did, except once a year on mother's birthday. ' Oh Angie,' a beaming mother would say, 'it's so good of you to come. I know you're such a busy girl. What would I do without you?' Sylvia would smile at nothing in particular.
Hollow days.

And then mother died and they carried her away. Sylvia opened the kitchen window wide and inhaled the soft Spring air. Her body softened and her hands trembled.

In April 1990 she stood at her mother's graveside. Her dark red hair was tied back from force of habit. She had not brought flowers and she knew she would never come again. She took a packet of cigarettes from her pocket and lit one. She inhaled deeply, then exhaled slowly, very slowly in the direction of her mother's headstone. She felt completely empty.

Sylvia needed to find a job—anything would do. She had no qualifications to speak of but an advertisement in the Post Office caught her eye. 'Companion wanted for an elderly woman. Good rates of pay.' She supposed she could do that and at least her evenings and weekends would be free.

She was interviewed by Miss Hinkley, a tall woman with crinkly silver hair and a probing expression. 'Well, Sylvia, you look like a nice dependable young woman. I think we'll get on fine.' Sylvia said she hoped they would. 'Oh, and I hope you can cook to my liking,' said Miss Hinkley, ' I'm very particular, you know. The last girl was so slovenly in the kitchen. I had to …' Sylvia's thoughts leapt far and away and she wondered if she was doing the right thing.

Every morning Sylvia woke at 7.30, had breakfast then dressed for work. Her wardrobe was small— there was little to choose from. Nowhere to go anyway. But now she was earning, she could save up. Yes, a very pleasing thought. Lastly she slipped into her trusted brown faux-suede jacket and left her house to begin the thirty minute walk to Miss Hinkley's.

By the end of the first week, Miss Hinkley invited Sylvia to call her Grace, 'After all we're friends now,' said Miss Hinkley.

'Yes of course,' said Sylvia as her fingers tightened Miss Hinkley's shoe laces.

'Ooh, that's too tight Sylvia. I'm not going to fall out of them now am I?'

'I was just trying to—'

'And please try to remember I have a delicate stomach. You put too much cheese into the sauce yesterday.'

Every day when Sylvia had completed her chores she would take up the newspaper, and because Grace's eyes tired easily these days, she would read her snippets of news—current affairs or something from the gossip column. But Sylvia soon became irritated by Grace's bigoted opinions and struggled to find an acceptable response. She knew her role was becoming uncomfortably familiar, but the weekends were hers alone. She began to make changes at home. It was her house now. Her rules. Her decisions. She felt dizzy with the endless possibilities. She uncluttered the living room and made plans to decorate the whole house. She would calm the walls by painting over the dated wallpaper and introduce some interesting leafy plants. The sofa and chairs needed recovering but she wasn't into that—she'd think of something.

Afternoons with Grace were easier. Sylvia loved the outdoors and enjoyed working in the garden while Grace sat in a wicker chair by the kitchen door and watched her. Actually Sylvia was an excellent gardener; she had helped her father as he tended their back garden. He taught her the names of all the shrubs and flowers. She had learnt about soils and when to plant and prune. And so she slowly transformed the tired lifeless garden into one of vibrant blues and purples with glossy leaves and delicately formed ferns.

'Careful with the yellow rose, Sylvia,' said Grace one day, 'my Thomas planted that and I'd be very sad if—' Sylvia grabbed the stem and wrenched it out of the ground. She hardly noticed as the dying bush embedded its thorns into the palm of her hand. Dark red mingled with the brown earth. Grace struggled to her feet, 'Why, Sylvia... My rose... Thomas...'

Sylvia threw the bush onto the compost heap. ' No Grace. It's diseased. We must get rid of it.' Grace's hands fluttered in the air and she sank back into her chair.

'Ooh. Well, if you say so. But I ...'

This small act of defiance made Sylvia's cheeks glow as a frisson of pleasure shot through her.

But what on earth had she done? Why hadn't she explained that the bush was diseased, talk her round a bit before... She was a fool that's why. Grace would probably sack her now. And she needed this job. She gathered her gardening tools and put them away in the shed and stood back as Grace silently made her way into the house. Sylvia felt sure she'd be asked to leave because Grace was clearly subdued, and so she hovered in the doorway unsure what expression to wear or where to put herself. 'Grace, I'm—' and then she stopped as Grace held up her hand. 'Sylvia, I'll just have a sandwich—ham will do—as I'm not feeling too good. You can leave it on my table. I don't want a meal tonight. I shall see you in the morning.'

Sylvia felt relief as she walked home. But that small act of defiance was firmly settled as any seed she'd planted in Grace's garden.

'Morning, Grace,' said Sylvia as she arrived the next morning. 'It's a fine day, would you like to go for a walk?'

'Actually Sylvia, I meant to mention something yesterday. What do you see on that skirting board?'

' I can see chipped paint,' said Sylvia as she followed Grace's pointing finger.

'Exactly. You really do need to take more care with the vacuum cleaner … You can be careless in your own home but not in mine.'

Sylvia flushed with fury but kept her voice strong and steady, 'Grace, I noticed the chipped paint on my first day here. I'm always careful with the vacuum cleaner. It certainly wasn't me.'

'Hmm. Very well, but I could have sworn …'

Sylvia bristled away her fury and brightened her face. 'Right Grace, shall we take a walk now?

'Maybe when you've read the paper to me. And don't read so fast today. It's a bad habit you have.'

Sylvia inhaled deeply, but she said nothing and picked up the newspaper and sat in her chair. As she re-positioned the cushion, her hand felt something papery; it was a ten pound note. Was she testing her? Oh my God, she was, wasn't she? Well, she'd show her. 'Oh look Grace,' said Sylvia as she held up the note, 'this must be yours. I wonder how it found its way behind the cushion on my chair?'

Grace wriggled and her face grew pink. 'Ohh ... Yes ... Silly me. I remember now. Last night I was going through my purse, looking for stamps and ... I ... I must have been sitting in your chair. Yes, that's it.'

'Right, Grace,' Sylvia could hear the directness in her own voice, 'about that walk. We'll go now—the newspaper can wait. You'll only need a jacket, it's a lovely day. Here's your stick and grab my arm.'

'Careful young lady. Don't get uppity with me—I'm paying you remember. I'll decide what I want to do.'

Sylvia stood her ground. 'Yes, and it's my job to encourage a little exercise every day. You know it's good for you.'

Grace grumbled her way into her jacket and took Sylvia's arm.

She endured a sleepless night. Mother's voice invaded her peace and trampled small victories: Woolworth's is good enough for you... Don't go getting any grand ideas—leave them to your sister. Sylvia fought to silence the voice; but the more she tried the more it filled her head, leaving no room for rest, no room for hope. She needed fresh air. She left her bed and opened her window and a predawn chill made her gasp. Glowing rectangles pierced the night as two, then three lights were flicked on in neighbouring houses. She supposed they heralded early workers quietly preparing for the day ahead. Or maybe fretful babies needing a parent's arms. She wanted to be part of that, wanted to be part of something; to feel the comfort of belonging. She was forty two years old and friendless. There had been no sunshine in her life since her father died. 'Don't take it to heart, Sylvie love,' he had always said, 'your mother can be a bit sharp at times—it's just her way. I'm sure she loves you though.'

The next few months held little inspiration for Sylvia, but she developed a forceful voice of reason and frequently used this to bat away any of Grace's unreasonable demands. Until she couldn't be bothered anymore. 'No, Grace,' she said one day as she plonked herself on the sofa, 'not today. I'm tired.'

'Oh... But you said I must take a short walk every—'

'Well, you can walk up and down the garden path a few times...Don't need me for that.' Sylvia turned on the TV and put her feet up, 'Ah, that's better.'

Grace grew very agitated, 'Sylvia—your feet...on my best...

'Oh, honestly! My shoes are off. What possible harm can my clean feet do to your precious sofa? The one that nobody actually sits on.'

But I—'

'Calm down, Grace—watch a bit of TV. Better than the boring old newspaper. Eh?'

'If you say so, but I don't usually watch—'

Sylvia raised her voice and liked the sound of it, 'That's enough! I know what's best for you. Nobody else would put up with your whingeing. Be grateful you've got me.'

Grace flinched. She tightened her lips and her face grew sullen.

One morning as Sylvia flicked through the pages of The Herald to find the TV listings, she spotted an advert for Adult Education Classes at Hamilton Sixth Form College. She paused. Well why not? Could be the very thing... Could get me out of this...

At home that evening, she read closely: 'Guitar for Beginners'—no, that wouldn't do. She'd be hopeless wouldn't she? And anyway was she really that interested? No. Moving on she hovered over 'Still Life Painting', but abandoned that thought when her eyes fixed on 'Soft Furnishings'. Was she ready for this? Yes she was. Her head was filled with colours, fabrics and yarns. Lime green and turquoise cushions would transform her dowdy living room; while her bedroom would welcome quiet greys and pinks. She noted the enrolment day—one week away. Yes, she was ready.

She stood outside the college on the opposite side of the road, taking in the red brick facade and its imposing dimensions. People were coming and going; they strode confidently and with purpose. Sylvia's resolve shrank a little. Her clammy hands balled in her pockets. But she didn't turn away.

Standing in the grand hall, she was overwhelmed by its size. She smiled to conceal her anxiety, but her darting eyes gave her away. 'Hello, can I help you?' asked a middle-aged man with a smooth face and lots of brown hair, 'you look rather lost.'

'I… I'm looking for the Soft Furnishings table,' said Sylvia, 'I'm new to all this you see.'

'Follow me then. Miss Sally Roberts will take care of you.'

Sylvia was led away to the far side of the hall, where she was introduced to the tutor. Her eyes swept over the display of photos. There were exquisitely crafted cushions and throws; samples of gem-coloured fabrics, muted yarns and patterns, some floral, others geometric. But most of all she was captivated by Sally Roberts: the warmth of her smile and her stylishness. Short, sleek black hair framed her fine features. A broad, black shiny belt and a jumble of ruby red beads around her neck. Sylvia was shockingly aware of her own frumpishness, of her functional don't-look-at-me clothes. Where was her imagination, for goodness sake? Held back—denied even, for too many years. Now, what was she waiting for? Her enrolment was now complete, and Sylvia promised herself a trip to Cole's department store. She would go the next day, Saturday.

She opened the doors to Cole's and went inside. She had never been before. There was no need. She climbed the stairs to the second floor; ahead of her a full-length mirror displayed her unflattering navy skirt and washed-out blouse. She supposed they did this on purpose; there was a very strong whiff of 'See how you need to buy something new' about the place but she chose to ignore it. She wanted a dress. When had she last worn one? A soft deep green caught her eye. She would try it on. The light in the cubicle flickered annoyingly so she pulled back the curtain for a better look. A sales assistant was at her side instantly. 'I think you need a smaller size, Madam. See how it bags at the waist and hips. And, why not try it in mid blue to bring out the blueness of your eyes. They're very blue aren't they?'

Compliments were rare—and Sylvia mistrusted them, but on this occasion ... it seemed to be true. 'Why... Yes, I suppose they are.' She disappeared into the cubicle. The dress was shorter than she was used to, but its full skirt swirled elegantly around her legs and accentuated her small waist. She felt a little giddy with the silliness of it all. But she liked what she saw in the mirror.

Sylvia looked forward to her Tuesday evening class when she could become someone else—the new Sylvia. Was this the real Sylvia? She felt it was. Hidden away— trapped even: walled in behind the facade of low expectations and dutiful diligence.
Good riddance!

She amazed herself by how quickly she learnt new skills, new techniques. But most of all it was the joy of belonging. She bought herself a sewing machine. She bought dozens of fabric remnants: muted tartans, mohair, silks and fine velvets. She bought decorative pieces in rose gold, emerald green and swirls of turquoise. Her evenings and weekends were happy ones and her home became a creative blur as her fingers busied themselves. She gazed at her cushions and was proud.

She ignored Grace's sullen face and random accusations. 'Do you know anything about my pearl earrings, Sylvia? They're missing and I'm not going to steal my own earrings, now am I ...?'

Blah, blah, blah-di-blah... You're gonna miss me, was Sylvia's silent response. Grace would be sorry alright.

Sylvia rented a market stall. Her cushions were in great demand—and so was she: the other traders loved her easy charm and creative flair.

'Put the red velvet aside for me, Sylvie. Pay you later,' said the neighbouring potter, 'Oh, and when you've got time I'd love that one in lime green with navy piping.'

Now she belonged.

At 9 o'clock every morning Grace would sit at her front room window. She would check her watch and click her tongue. She was probably looking for Sylvia. But Sylvia never returned.

A Murder of Crows

The month of May was fading: lilacs, once heady and heavily plumed, had now lost their vibrant hue and plump clusters; they bowed their heads knowingly, awaiting the end.

In the watery, grey, morning light, Marion Mutter stepped outside into the wilderness that was her garden. She did not tend this mass of tangled weeds and discarded household items, for the simple reason that she was never outdoors long enough to bring any significant sense of order to this abandoned piece of land. She scurried to the bin, raised a clenched fist to the skies as she yelled dark oaths, and then retreated to her kitchen where she continued to gesticulate from behind the window-panes.

The trouble lay skyward; well, to be more accurate, trouble lay in the branches of the tall coniferous trees that stood behind Marion's cottage.

Crows.

Those damned feathered creatures, arrogant in their coal-black sleekness, perched high to deliver their raucous cries, their dry rattling call that invaded her day and boiled her blood. Oh, how she loathed them. If a single winged enemy should venture into her garden, its ungainly strut and clever eye would send her railing and stamping out of her back door until it flew off to a more favourable landing place.

Yes, Marion hated the sound and sight of crows more than spending money: to Marion, a penny spent was a penny wasted. Her poor house shivered through many a cold winter—heating cost money and she was mean and tough enough to do without. She simply shrugged off the chill by stuffing a few layers of old newspapers into her clothing. Clothing so ancient that it had lost any identifiable hue and consisted almost entirely of random patches and ugly darns. And as for food ...

A small handful of pound coins would be sufficient to meet her weekly shopping bill.

Only the staples would be allowed entry into her basket: potatoes headed the bill—to be fried, baked, roasted or boiled. Eggs came a close second, so versatile and not to be beaten for food value. Coming up in third place was usually a large head of Savoy cabbage: just delicious when shredded, fried or steamed to perfection. There were never any leftovers.

Now, Miss Mutter badly needed to solve the problem of the offending birds—teach them a lesson. She mused on the subject for many days and nights. At last her thoughts turned to a more violent nature: she would make her very own catapult and slay the lot of them, one by one. She discovered a forked, oak twig near the dustbin and began to fashion it into her weapon of choice. Next she needed a target. She spent a happy morning creating a cloth bird out of bits snipped from the hem of her black skirt, and for glue she mixed flour with a little of the liquid used to boil the remains of a dead pigeon. When ready, she pinned the target to a wall in her front room, and took pleasure in driving the tack through the eye of her creation. As soon as a sturdy rubber band and a marble were found, Marion began target practice. She closed her right eye and stuck out her yellowed tongue in readiness. Clumsy and way off the mark at first, she eventually mastered the technique and admired her new found skill, oblivious to marks peppered over the wall and time spent removing her ammunition from ageing holes in her dusty cushions. And so, with a marble and catapult at hand, she awaited victim number one.

For two days she kept a very close eye on her garden— watching hawk-like for any landings. Nothing.

And then there it was, out of the corner of her eye she caught sight of a streak of blackness as it swooped down and landed ceremoniously at the foot of the cobbled path, where it paused to survey possibilities. But Marion's hand was quick to find her weapon, position herself in the doorway, take aim and fire. A dull thwack filled the air as a tiny trickle of crimson blood stilled the sleek, black feathers. Marion dived back into her kitchen, triumphant and feeling intoxicated with happiness but wanting to escape the inevitable screeching as they mourned one of their own.

Ten loaded seconds went by before the cacophony began: murderous yet awesome in its enormity; it was an outpouring of grief, of rage, from every one of the assembling crows. Marion covered her ears with her hands as she stamped her feet to block out the swelling noise. Possibly ten minutes went by; she released a hand but clamped it back immediately. Still there. Still there. Weary of stamping, she sank into her armchair and caught sight of the headphones newly rescued from a skip. Once in place, although slightly misshapen and clearly having seen better days, they provided the perfect defence. 'Knew they'd come in handy,' said Miss Mutter, addressing the air of her cluttered front room.

The remains of the day went like a dream. Headphones effectively installed, she pledged to keep them on, night and day, as she went about her chores and musings; her thoughts now uninterrupted, her blood calmed.

Early next morning, Marion stepped outside her kitchen door to breathe in the new day. Of course, she hadn't heard the mass gathering of crows, their rallying cries of kraa, kraa, kraa; she hadn't known that they recognise faces; that they will seek revenge. They swooped. A heaving mass of blackness; brutal beaks stripping away life. No one heard her strangled cries. Mercifully, death came swiftly; death was her saviour.

A murder of crows.

The Bracelet

Annie rarely went up to town, but maybe that was about to change. The interview, she felt, had gone well: she'd fed them exactly what they wanted to hear and made them believe she was the *only* person for the job. She allowed herself a few moments of pleasurable scenarios: Lunches with her husband, Dougie. Well occasionally, perhaps. He'd been so very busy for the past six months; she'd lost count of the wasted dinners. Not that she minded cooking them—she was always home first. Then when he eventually arrived home he would say apologetically, *So sorry but I grabbed a bite earlier. I tell you what, tomorrow I'll be home early and I'll cook.* It rarely happened.

She was way too early for her train; she had a couple of hours to spare before she needed to head back to Waterloo station. Okay, it was late morning so maybe she could meet Dougie for lunch, she could be in the City in fifteen minutes by tube. Yes, it would be a treat for them both. She sent a text and hovered around the shops at Kings Cross whilst she waited for a reply. She let out a disappointed sigh when she read his text. *Sorry. No time for lunch—I'm working through. Will try to get back early X.* Oh well. She suddenly thought of Russell Square gardens—such an oasis of calm and she hadn't been there for years. She bought coffee and a sandwich and hurried in that direction.

The day was mild and the sky a dim grey: the type of sky that was so blank it sapped any purity of colour from everything below it. But as Annie walked along the horseshoe path in search of somewhere to sit, her pace slowed and she stood still. In front of her sat a woman with a head of glorious auburn hair—a bright beacon of deep orange-red. Annie moved towards her, drawn by its beauty. The bench was long and the woman sat at one end with her head bowed as she read from a book. She looked up briefly as Annie sat down, and as she did so revealed blue-violet eyes and pale, freckled skin. Annie looked away as she sipped her coffee but her thoughts remained with the woman at the far end of the bench and she wondered why she found her presence so compelling. Did she remind her of anyone? A neighbour or ex-colleague? What about cousin Florence—she'd not seen her for ages. No, this woman was too young. Nobody sprang to mind. But what was it? She supposed the woman was in her early thirties—a good ten or fifteen years younger than she was. But why did she *matter*? She was just a woman sitting on a bench, for goodness sake. Annie was beginning to feel slightly uneasy but she had no idea why. She didn't know the person sitting next to her, she was no obvious threat and extremely unlikely to stick a knife in her ribs. Annie shook her head, sat up straight and rearranged her coat as she brushed away bothersome thoughts.

She bit into her sandwich as a sparkle caught her eye. She turned. The woman raised her hand to replace a stray lock of hair, and in doing so revealed a silver bracelet inlaid with teardrop shaped rubies—a perfect match for her brilliant hair. Annie struggled to swallow as her stomach lurched and the breeze stilled. 'If you don't mind me saying, that's a beautiful bracelet and such an unusual design. In fact… In fact I have one just like that, only mine has emeralds.'

'Yes,' replied the woman, as a warm smile lit up her face, 'it's gorgeous isn't it.' The bracelet became hidden again in the sleeve of her coat as she returned to her book, but its image was firmly planted in Annie's mind. She knew she should finish her lunch and go: leave the bench, the woman and the bracelet behind—she *wanted* to go. She wanted to get on with her day, get on with her life, but she couldn't. Some inner force was keeping her there and she was compelled to find out why.

'Excuse me, I'm sorry to interrupt but your bracelet intrigues me. Was it made to your design?'

'No, oh no,' said the woman as she turned to face Annie, 'it was a gift… From my boyfriend, actually.'

'Oh, I see. Was it his design, do you know? Or the silversmith's?'

'To be honest I don't know, but I love it and it never leaves my wrist. What about yours?

'Oh, it was a gift from my husband… A twentieth wedding anniversary gift.' Annie breathed rapidly as she recalled the day: 'Dougie, it's beautiful.' The green gems winked as he fastened the bracelet onto her wrist and replied, 'My design, you know.'

Now she wished she had worn it today—to compare… But no, not the thing for an interview, a bit too showy she felt. She must stop. She was delving too deep. She must go no further. Stay on the surface. Stay safe. Just finish the sandwich and leave.

'I don't normally come here, there's never enough time,' said the woman. 'It's just that I have the day off… Wanted some fresh air——a bit of me time, you know. But most importantly I actually get to have lunch with my boyfriend. We work in the same company but rarely get the chance to leave the building at the same time. You know how it is…'

Annie kept digging, despite the warning signs: her breath quickened and she sat rigidly still, so still in a hopeless effort not to be harmed. 'Where …Where do you work?'

'Mayland Brothers, in the city,'replied the woman. Annie's world suddenly blurred. The woman's hair lost its vibrant glow and became garishly untouchable—a burning emblem of danger, and her eyes took on a callous hue of iron-grey.

'Ohh… I…,' said Annie and as her jaw tightened she stopped, looked away and watched as her sandwich fell to the ground.

'Er, are you OK?' asked the woman, 'only you don't look too well. Is it something I said—'

Annie's hand shot up. 'No, no absolutely not. I must be having an off day. That's all.'

'And look,' said the woman, 'you've dropped your lunch.'

'Oh, that,' she replied as she kicked the fallen sandwich under the bench, 'It really doesn't matter.'

The woman reached into her bag and pulled out a muesli bar. 'Here, have this. I always carry one—just in case.'

Annie turned and inwardly recoiled; the outstretched hand might as well have held a grenade. Do not touch. Get away now. You have been warned. But her legs refused to move. Boneless now. 'No. Thank you but I'm not that hungry.' She closed her lips very tightly as she struggled to contain and forbid the words that had formed in her head. She failed. They tumbled out and hung in the air, as a prisoner awaits sentencing. 'Have... Have you been together for long... Er, with your boyfriend, I mean?'

'Not that long. Six months actually. But you just *know*, don't you when you find *the one*.'

'Well, I suppose... Yes of course you do... Do you, do you plan to marry? Oh I'm sorry... I shouldn't ask—'

'Oh it's fine. It's good to share happiness, and yes we intend to marry just as soon as Dougie is divorced.' She looked at her watch. 'I must fly. Got to meet him for lunch. Bye. Nice to meet you.'

Annie gripped the bench and tried to stay upright as the stream of scarlet hair rippled its way out of the gardens.

Heavy Stones

Eric's glasses were missing. He searched high and low, retraced his steps, but still they remained hidden from view. He knew he was in deep trouble because he couldn't see a damned thing without them. He sat down and thought really hard about the situation, but found that too difficult without his glasses. Oh pah.

Just then he remembered and cursed himself for being so slow. Of course! There was a spare pair in the front room—they'd been there for years. He reached for them in the cupboard and sighed with relief. He turned. His father's piano stood in the corner by the window. He lifted the lid and his fingers rippled along the keys; the tone was still good. It's all about the tone, his father had said. As Eric settled on the stool, the notes flowed and released his childhood days. He played his father's favourite, 'In the Good Old Summer Time', badly at first but soon the music and images were as one.

1905

When hard frosts and cruel winds heralded January, the young Eric had wondered what he might receive for his birthday. He really, really wanted a hobby-horse just like his best friend Johnnie had, but he didn't think he'd be that lucky. But he was. He raced downstairs on his birthday and there it was, a red and blue hobby-horse with a mane of bright yellow wool.

Eric and Johnnie journeyed far and wide. In the Wild West they herded cattle and chased rustlers across the Plains. They travelled through time, riding with heroes and heroines. Armed with silver swords and fearsome courage, they battled with red-eyed monsters and yellow-backed demons who spewed fire and venom across the land. And always their trusty steeds would carry them safely home.

He played on. The music shifted from urgent and sonorous to distant and haunting as strains of 'Hungarian Rhapsody' filled the air. He lifted his head. The window revealed the mid-day glare of the summer sun's shimmering heat. And then it came: the sunlit hell of the Somme; and with it that familiar feeling like a heavy stone moving around his inside.

July 1916

The very first day had been the bloodiest. As the whistles blew, Eric and Johnnie shook hands as they always did before going over-the-top. Sweat glistened on their faces. Fear was a constant enemy. Johnnie went first. Never had a chance. Struck down as he showed above the parapet. Eric caught his friend as he fell back. Saw the gaping hole where his belly had been. Saw the face he knew so well with its big toothy grin, now distorted in agony. Saw the bright brown eyes, now brimming with horror, become vacant—black holes. Nothing. Eric held Johnnie's bloodied hand and watched as his friend's last brave breath spluttered and died, 'Eri...'

'Move it Thompson!' came the order.

Huge black shells screamed down. Shouts of torment and calls for help from all around. Dying men shrieked terrible curses. Eric saw the young lad from down his street just kneeling as bullets plunged into him, knocking great bloody pieces off his body. They cried for their God. He never came.

Wracked with grief and blinded by tears, Eric went forward into the black dust. Into hell. No choice.

Why on earth had he let Johnnie go first? They were supposed to go together; that was always the plan. Had Johnnie known— had he sensed the end? Known chances of survival were zero? He had hadn't he? He'd wanted to save his friend. And he'd abandoned Johnnie in the trench. Had to leave his poor shattered body for comrades to trample on as they surged forward. Johnnie's blood and gore on their boots. Why hadn't he called 'Wait Johnnie.' What had he been doing? Why had he survived? And then telling Johnnie's mother. Seeing her face crumple; her scream had pierced his heart. What was left of it.

Why my Johnnie? No ... no, not my Johnnie .... No—

Did she hate him? Of course she did. What sort of a friend was he? He was a coward. That's why he'd let Johnnie go first.

Survivor's guilt would haunt him forever. Heavy stones moving around his inside.

He paused for a few minutes then found the keys once more: the soulful sound nudged his thoughts towards Iris. The image of her was still quite perfect in his mind. There was no need for a framed bedside photograph—no need at all—for he recalled her face every day of his life. But just in case the unthinkable should happen, that someday her image would fade, become uncertain, he had a photo of her carefully stored away in a little wooden chest. But for now his memory held safe her tawny complexion and watchful brown eyes: eyes that could scold and melt in a heartbeat. Iris, headstrong and proud; strong-limbed with fingers that twitched and intertwined when she was nervous. Iris. The woman who had tried to heal his pain. The woman who had given him a reason to live and held him through his darkest nightmares.

Why had she fallen for him? He was never quite sure. He thought himself too tall, really: his whole upper body seemed to drift and sway as if he might topple over on a wild and windy day. His long feet made him look kind of L-shaped. They got in the way; they tripped people up; they stuck out at the bottom of every bed he had ever slept in. And as for shoes! When he was actually lucky enough to find a pair large enough to house his oversized extremities, they were, needless to say, twice the price of 'normal' shoes and seriously lacking in style and comfort. Iris would sigh in resignation, 'Eric, your feet...'

Her brown walking boots still sat next to his in the back porch. Mud still caked in the treads. He had no desire to clean them: didn't want to wash away their last hike together in August 1955. And so the boots sat side by side, a constant and necessary reminder of that hot summer in the Lake District where they'd scaled Scafell and swam in the cool, cool tarns. Where they'd filled themselves with the freedom and beauty of the landscape. Where they lay breathless and fulfilled under the vast and vivid blue sky.

And because his legs were so long, Eric had to sleep with his feet sticking out of their small tent. He liked to sleep with his feet bare, and so from time to time a bothersome tickling from little night creatures would wake him. A quick twitch and repositioning of the troublesome feet did the trick. 'Put your boots on,' Iris would say, 'then they won't bother you. Or buy a bigger tent, for goodness sake.' He never did.

They had waited a long time for Gerry, their son. His arrival had been such a joyous occasion, particularly for Iris who had begun to believe that she would remain childless. But along came Gerry, a beautiful strong-willed child who did not have, thankfully, Eric's enormous feet.

Eric was aware that some days he fell short of being the father he had wanted to be. A sudden smell could provoke a vivid and disturbing memory. His temper would flare then vanish as he withdrew entirely into himself. Iris would arrive as Gerry's little face crumpled into big tears. She would scoop him up and distract him with some messy baking activity or ball game. Eric loathed himself then. Loathed himself until Iris found him again and brought him back from the abyss of hell.

He could never pinpoint the start of her illness, but he became aware of changes in her personality: subtle at first but soon very obvious. The menopause perhaps? Iris's mood would change from pink to blue in a heartbeat—for no apparent reason. No terrible news or disappointment; no sudden decline in the weather. Nothing out of the ordinary. She would turn silent and sullen; drop out of a conversation. 'Whatever you say Eric... I can't be bothered.' And her eyelids would lower; her face shuttered against the world.

Eric watched helplessly as Iris gradually lost interest in the things she loved. 'Eric, get a gardener... or no... do it yourself,' she said one day as she stormed in from the garden, 'I'm sick of battling with weeds and cleaning that bloody pond—again.'

'I thought you loved being out there,' said Eric, 'What's changed?... Thought it was your haven...'

Iris snatched off her gardening gloves and hurled them across the kitchen where they landed—depositing loose soil—on the newly baked ginger cake. Eric stilled his mounting concern and with a smile that didn't quite reach his eyes, guided Iris away from the kitchen.

Later he ran out in the rain to collect the abandoned gardening tools and placed them in the shed. Something that Iris had always done. For a few moments he enjoyed the fat raindrops as they splashed on his upturned face. Welcomed the distraction from his growing unease.

They had always enjoyed entertaining friends: good food, lively conversation and a warm atmosphere. But

Eric began to feel Iris's discomfort and impatience. She would become tense and argumentative—aggressive even. Friends would exchange tell-tale sideways glances and widen their eyes. 'Shut up Eric,' said Iris one evening, in an increasingly loud voice, 'just shut up. That's a load of bullshit and you know it.' She slapped the table, upsetting a carafe of wine that turned the crisp white cloth into a deep blushing pink and left the cheese floundering helplessly on its board.

'Right you two lovely people, we must be on our way now,' said the startled friends, 'early start and all that...'

No farewell hugs and kisses; just a tight 'thanks' and then they'd gone.

'Well, that was rude of them,' said Iris, 'we hadn't even finished the meal. Ah well, who cares. It's all too much trouble.'

Eric started to clear the mess from the table then paused and in a quiet voice said, 'You know Iris, perhaps we should make an appointment to see Dr. Young. You're just not yourself these days.'

'Nonsense!' said Iris with a swipe of her hand, 'everyone gets fed up at times.'

Eric knew differently. He was, by now, used to her caustic tongue and careless ways. He sought help and advice. He desperately wanted to sooth her troubled mind.

He knew she had problems at work: she was no longer efficient, no longer reliable. She made mistakes and forgot important information. Tongues wagged. She was taken aside. 'Can I have a word, Iris?' But Iris couldn't understand what was wrong. Eric knew they would elbow her out and he just couldn't bear to see her dismissed. In the end he persuaded her to take early retirement. 'More time for this and that, Iris. What about that novel you've always wanted to write?' Iris didn't answer, and anyway Eric knew that would never happen now. Heavy stones moving around his inside.

Soon after, Eric decided to hide the car keys—permanently—to protect Iris from herself, really. She had become confused about time and space. That innate ability to get from A to B, her wonderful sense of direction, had deserted her. 'Where've you been sweetheart? I was worried.'

'Well,' said an agitated Iris, 'I don't know... I just got a bit mixed up... Couldn't seem to find...'

The following day was the worst. The police brought her home in the early evening: she had been found wandering on the outskirts of town in a very distressed and dishevelled state. Her face was damp with tears and the terror in her eyes was like an arrow of fear in Eric's heart. He held her close and felt the rage in her heart. 'I couldn't remember where I'd parked the car... No, no it wasn't that... they've stolen it haven't they? They're all thieves... Call the police, Eric!'

It wasn't long before Eric realised that he must retire and care for Iris. She was deteriorating quite rapidly now and couldn't be left on her own for more than an hour or so. His latest trip to the local shops had proved to be costly. He smelt the smoke from the top of the street. Someone having a bonfire he supposed. Then the awful dawning: Oh my God! Iris—Please no. Bags dropped, legs ate the ground as he raced through the house and into the back garden and there she stood clapping her hands as precious books and items of clothing were engulfed in flames. 'Too many, too many, too many, too many,' sang Iris.

'No! Stop! Stop!' said Eric as his voice leapt above hers. He grabbed the hosepipe to quell the fire. Too late of course. The damage was done. Nothing salvageable: their books now sodden and charred. Chunks devoured by the ravenous flames. Her elegant dresses and his smart navy suits now shapeless lumps of charcoal. Iris slumped down on an old garden chair. Loose strands of pale hair lay limp across her face. She was defeated. Eric knew he had spoiled her fun.

He suddenly felt very lonely and completely overwhelmed by it all. He didn't recognise his wife. Who was this woman? Where was Iris? Little by little this progressive disease had crept in and stolen her personality, stolen her generosity of spirit. And yet he knew that the essence of the woman he loved was still there. Of course it was. He just had to step into her skin and move around a little. This was her world now: full of confusion, mistrust and restlessness. He wished her no harm, of course he didn't, but he longed for relief from the pain of seeing her suffer. No matter. He would bear it. Because it wasn't about him. Was it?

Mirrors had to be removed—all of them. Iris became very distressed at the sight of herself; a woman she no longer recognised. One day Eric found fragments of glass from the dressing table mirror lying on the path below the bedroom window. As he bandaged her lacerated hands she berated him: 'Who's that woman Eric? Tell me now. Get rid of her. I know you... you've got another woman living in my house.'

'There's no-one else. Just Iris,' said Eric as he kissed her poor hands and brushed smooth her still corn-coloured hair.

She became restless, so restless most of the time. He tried to find new things to keep her busy but she soon tired of them and tossed them aside. No focus. No interest. But she loved to hear him play the piano. It was the only time she seemed at ease with herself. She would sit quite still, hands steady on her lap and her face serene. He would play for an hour or more—'Moon River' and 'Too Marvellous For Words' were her favourites—only too happy to know her pleasure. And as he played he wondered where she went. Was it the journey of her youth? Or to another world, unimagined by him? And then her eyelids would droop and softly close. She would sleep awhile. Eric would slip away from the piano and lie down, freeing his mind and body and think of nothing except the serenity of the colour blue.

Aged just fifty eight, Iris passed away on a cold winter's day. Eric's grief was all-consuming. Giant waves of sadness would engulf him, take away his breath until he almost drowned in sorrow. But he would never deny a sense of relief. Her death was untimely but her torment, so devastating. So unforgiving.

What was it she'd once said? You never really lose someone Eric. It's all about the love they leave behind.

She was so right wasn't she. But what about him? Had he loved her enough? Had he cared enough when her mind had gone? He felt sure he hadn't. What made him think he'd deserved her? Heavy stones moving around his inside.

Tears clouded his vision. The keys blurred and swam in front of him as he lost himself to her memory. They said grief would lessen in time, but that was a lie just to make you feel better. Time hadn't made him feel better at all. How could they possibly know that his hollowed heart would heal? They couldn't know because they were not Eric Thompson.

So lost was he that he didn't hear his son Gerry, turn a key in the front door. He didn't hear his young grandson burst in, 'Hello Grandpa, I'm here.' He didn't know until he felt the small boy clambering up onto the piano stool beside him, his beaming face and those big brown eyes—Iris's eyes—shining up at him. 'Play for me, Grandpa.'

Eric smiled, for he knew that this small child would break his sorrow. Heal his heart.

Watling Street

Mild impatience eventually gave way to a full blown rage as Kezia got out of her car, slammed the door and belted the bonnet with her shopping bag time and time again until her fury subsided. Oh how easy it is, she mused, to rail against the incompetence of… a lump of metal. Well, now she would have to walk; there was no time to wait for assistance because she needed to check on her father as promised. She delved into her bag for her gloves but found they were sopping wet with orange juice that had exploded from its carton when she was thrashing the car. Kezia sighed heavily. 'That'll teach me to check out my weapon of choice before laying into… Ah well, it's only about a mile and a half.'

A damp, still, greyness heralded an evening fog; if she walked quickly she would be there in twenty five or thirty minutes. But the invader fell thick and fast; familiar surroundings rapidly became unfamiliar. Her footfall became less sure as she adjusted her scarf to cover her nose and mouth in an attempt to keep out the thickening night. She stopped to make a circling movement. As she lifted her head and strained her eyes she could just make out chimney pots, but they were parted from their roofs as if floating on a murky sea. She knew she was lost. As she held out a hand in front of her, that too soon became a shapeless blur, swallowed up by the invading gloom.

Gloveless and hatless, she felt the gripping chill bite her fingers and the cloak of fog rendered her short, fine hair an icy cap that numbed her brain. Strained eyes betrayed her sense of direction as Kezia, not daring to let herself loose on the pavement, or cross a road for fear of a vehicle suddenly looming out of the thick grey shroud, clung to the solidness of a brick wall as she inched her way forward. Forward to where? Feeling in her pocket for her phone, but finding it empty, urged her brain into action. Her mind's eye efficiently searched her home. Yes, she knew exactly where her phone was; it was lying next to the fridge where she had left it, innocently awaiting instructions. Now her Dad would wonder where she was.

The roads became clear of traffic. It had been several minutes since a pair of struggling headlamps had stoically passed her by. Having been tricked and robbed of her bearings, Kezia was temporarily fooled into thinking that familiar places ceased to exist, changed identity and had become deliberately hostile to her needs. Trick of the imagination? Maybe. A niggling anxiety took hold as the fog crept and lurked: grey faced and damp as it captured its prey and molested all that lay in its wake, permeating mind and body. She cried out as something raked through her hair. She froze, unable to move expecting a hand to her throat—or worse. But no, it was just the overhanging branches of a naked tree.

Her hand fell from the wall as she turned, ears alerted to the distant sound of footsteps; her heart quickened as they approached. She sensed they came from the opposite side of the road. 'Hello there,' she called. And again her voice leapt into the night, 'Hello.' As the footsteps slowed she expected a response but none came. Her shoulders drooped as she realised once more that she was alone. All she could hear was the chilled quietness of her breath.

Too cold to stand still, her hand felt for the wall again as she moved on in the hope of making out a street sign or a familiar corner. Where were the street lamps? Her eyes strained: searching, searching for guidance. And there it was, a dim light escaping from the cracks between curtains. She edged her way up an uneven path until she reached a large front door. Surely now she could seek help. She knocked several times, each time louder than the last until her knuckles felt bruised. No one came. No one came for fear of that unwanted visitor slipping in and stealing their cosiness. Disappointment turned her away. What now? She had no idea how far she had travelled. How can you tell when your pace is so hesitant and slow, when your steps are so small and the night a steep bank of fog, barring your way. A dogged spirit urged her forward with the hope of another light, another chance to seek help.

She arrived at the corner of an end of terraced houses. And not wishing to cross a road, turned left and bumped straight into the solid form of... a man. 'Oh, how you st... I'm so sorry,' said Kezia as her heart drummed and her hand leapt to her chest, 'I don't suppose you have a phone I could use, only my father will be worried and—'

'Slow down, slow down,' replied the man who gently touched her arm as if to calm, to soothe. 'I expect you're lost and it's a dreadful night to be out. Maybe I can help?'

A tsunami of relief washed over Kezia as she looked up at the man who stood just a few centimetres away from her. Peering through the gloom she could make out an older, kindly face. 'Well, I'm trying to get to Watling Street to check on my father and yes I'm hopelessly lost and I've stupidly left my phone at home.'

'I see,' said the man, 'you're about a mile from Watling Street but I live at the other end of this terrace, so you're welcome to use my phone—mine's at home too I'm afraid, and let your father know you're safe.'

'Oh, how kind, how kind.'

'And,' continued the man, 'I've nothing much to do this evening so I could guide you home or to wherever you want to be. I've got this very reliable sense of direction, you know...never lets me down. Follow me.'

Kezia's muscles relaxed as she walked alongside the man whose stride was heavy and long to her short, quick steps. After a couple of minutes he stopped and said, 'Here we are,' as he turned onto a little pathway that led to his front door. Kezia smiled up at him. Help was at hand. He locked eyes with her for a fraction of a second too long. Or did she just imagine that? Probably. He opened the door, switched on the light and stood aside to let Kezia into the hallway. 'Go straight ahead past the stairs, please.'

The sudden brightness of the light startled Kezia and she lowered her head to shield her eyes. When she looked up the man had removed his coat and hat and she was struck by his youthful appearance as he stood arms by his side wearing a smart, tan, corduroy suit. She had thought he was much older—how strange. He remained very still, and again locked eyes with her. She felt a nudge of discomfort. What was she thinking of? She would never normally enter a complete stranger's house like this. OK, these were not normal circumstances, but even so... 'Erm... if I could just borrow your phone, I'll be on my way.'

'Well now, I need to find it... now where did I put it?'

She eyed the landline phone and he saw her turn towards it. 'The line's dead, I'm afraid that's no use... I tell you what, let's have a nice cup of hot tea and *then* I'll find my mobile.'

'No thank you. If you could please—'

'Sit down,' said the man whose words hung in the air like threatening storm clouds, 'First we will have tea.'

The discomfort swelled within her, and as he moved into the kitchen she ran back down the hall, desperate now to flee out into the gloom once more. She tugged and turned at the latch and as she did so she saw a collage of images: her father sitting waiting for her; she saw her friends safe at home preparing their evening meals; she saw sunshine and laughter and she saw tomorrow. But the door was locked. Kezia's hand fell away and from behind her came his voice, now impatient, urgent even. 'I asked you to sit down. Now. I need to begin.'

And as he stepped towards her, there were no more images.

Third Turning on the Right

Eddie fell into a vacant seat as the train slid out of Kings Cross station. After an endless day he found the carriage warm and comforting, its motion hypnotic. Tense muscles relaxed, heavy eyelids flickered and closed. No matter. He would be awake before he reached his destination.

Obscure faces loomed then receded; distant voices tumbled through his mind as they played a wicked game, lurking round the edge of his subconscious. His arm flailed a little: some unsuccessful attempt at batting away the invaders. And then came a voice, persistent and loud, followed by a sharp nudge to his shoulder, 'End of the line, sir! Come on, let's be having you.'

Tumbling out from the fuggy atmosphere onto the platform, Eddie exhaled a long and steady groan: the type of groan that describes a deep, disappointing realisation. This was not Cambridge, his hometown, but some God forsaken place he'd heard of but never visited: King's Lynn. 'When's the next train back to Cambridge?' he called after the man in uniform.

'Nothing until 06.10, now mate," a cheerful voice replied.

Standing outside the station, Eddie paused to review his situation: he soon realised that a taxi was absolutely out of the question; Cambridge was too far away, and he didn't have enough money. His only option was to maybe find a lowly B&B—a bed for the night, any sort of bed would do, just somewhere willing to welcome his weariness for a few hours.

His footsteps fell heavy, matching the weight of his fatigue. A terrace of little houses, patched and down at heel, revealed no possibilities whatsoever; but he went forward; he wandered; he searched a town that seemed very closed for the night. As he turned corners, the mundane ordinariness gave way to imposing architecture: still grand in dimension—the hallmark of a once significant and prosperous town. Eventually he came upon its river, bleak, silent and wide. Stone alleyways leading down to it echoed their history of dark secrets captured in cold cobbles.

But this was hopeless. His thoughts scurried back to the urgent need of a bed. And so, with renewed vigour, he strode away from the waterfront when he spotted a pedestrian— hopefully a local. Eddie hurried now as he approached the man and made his inquiry. 'I can't think of any B&Bs off hand, but there's a couple of hotels round the corner on the square," came the thoughtful reply. 'No, wait a minute, there is a B&B I believe on the old coach road. Not much happening out there these days and it's a bit of a walk but I'm pretty certain it's still open for business. It's straight ahead, then the third turning on the right.'

'Thanks for your help,' said Eddie as he hurried forward.

His pace quickened as raindrops began to fall; big raindrops fell, thick and heavy, spiteful raindrops fell as they sensed his thin jacket, defenceless against such an invasion. And so he reached the edge of town weighed down with misery and rain. He calculated that he had reached the old coach road but could see no signs of life. His eyes scoured the darkness until he believed he could just make out a building maybe three hundred metres to the north. He ran now, so urgent was his need for rest. Yes! Yes! Yes! It was indeed a house, ramshackle as far as he could make out, but there in the window, sitting at a very rakish angle, was a sign, a most welcome sign: B&B vacancies.

A curtain twitched. A dull orange light spilled out into the night as the front door cracked open and at its edge crept a pair of tiny black eyes beneath a brillo pad of grey hair, and a voice said, 'Saw you coming.'

'I know it's very late but do you have a bed for the night?' asked Eddie whose hand clutched the doorframe as his voice rang out a little more desperate than intended.

'I'll let you have one for twenty quid cash. Bed only," said the voice.

Eddie rummaged in his pockets for he knew he had that amount—just about. His hands found a note and various coins which he placed in the outstretched hand; thin fingers grasped greedily as the door swung wide to allow the traveller in. Those tiny black eyes lay riveted on Eddie's face. And his host wore a smile; a smile that didn't belong: stolen perhaps.

'Your room's up here, follow me.' The steep and narrow staircase lay ahead; every few seconds the host would pause on a step, turn and fix the traveller with those black riveting eyes. Disconcerting to most, but not to a bone-tired Eddie. 'Bathroom's at the end there,' pointed a bony hand, 'we've a full house tonight so they'll be queuing in the morning, no doubt.'

Eddie had no interest in the room; the bed had seen healthier days, but it would do. He removed his sodden jacket and placed it on the back of a rickety dining chair, then with some pleasure allowed himself to drop onto the narrow bed. His final act before abandonment was to remove the ring of keys from his jeans pocket: the dragon shaped fob tended to cause discomfort and must be replaced.

A small cough emerged from Eddie's sleeping form. It was followed by another, then another. His body twitched and turned in an attempt to avoid the disturbance. Acrid fumes reached out, filling nostrils, throat and lungs, filling every available space until its toxins urged him awake. He leapt to his feet and instinctively covered his lower face as his burning lungs struggled to function. He knew the procedure: he covered his hand with his still damp jacket, stuffed his feet into his shoes, grabbed his keys and reached for the doorknob and turned. What lay on the other side rendered him momentarily petrified. A vicious furnace of raging flames licked and whorled ahead of him as it headed for the stairs, its roar blood-curdling and its orange plumes devouring all in its path. He knew he must move—now, like when your options are down to zero. He covered his head with the damp coat and leapt through the black wall of smoke that was the staircase. He landed in a heap in the hallway below. He was bruised, choking and shaking uncontrollably as he fumbled to open the front door and gasped as he inhaled the clean night air.

He tried very hard to call out, to warn the others: those who were still sleeping, but only a small strangled cry could be heard which was carried off by the wind. Eddie knew that he must raise the alarm. Find help—fire brigade—tell somebody. So he ran with a strength that came from deep within him; he would run until he could wake the sleeping town.

Retracing his steps back to the heart of the town, he scanned streets and alleyways for signs of wakefulness. And then he saw a pale light glowing from the first floor of a pub, *The Merchant's Rest*. He hammered on the door. 'Help! There's a fire!' A sash window was flung open and from above his head came the angry response, 'What the hell's going on? It's three in the morning!'

'There's a fire at the B&B on the old coach road. Can you call the fire brigade? Hurry. People are still in there.'

'Are you mad or what? There's no B&B out there, hasn't been for at least twenty years. Just a ruin... Never been touched. Now bugger off.'

The window slammed shut, even the panes rattled their annoyance. Eddie remained on the pavement, rooted to the spot, trying to make sense of what he had just heard. But no, he was very much awake and his lungs still stung with every breath he took. And so he turned on his heel and ran back to the old coach road. Maybe there was something he could do ... Before it was too late.

There was no furnace: no flames lit the night sky; no cries from within. He brushed aside the tall weeds: black bindweed, bramble and buddleia. He approached the ruin with slow, uncertain steps. Mullioned windows that once held stylish drapes were now gaping rectangles, laid bare for eternity. Eddie instinctively held

back—this was way too much. How could he possibly…
But he was urged forward by a force from… Somewhere
deep inside. Or was it? His shoulder pushed away the
charred remains of a front door. He looked up and
saw the sliver of moon. He could make out where the
staircase had been. He had leapt down on them just
a few hours ago, hadn't he? But that wasn't possible
was it? His foot kicked something as he turned: it
skidded a little way then came to rest. Eddie followed its
movement. He took a closer look. There in the rubble of
the ruin lay his keys with the dragon shaped fob.

Hell Hath No Fury

Katia had just celebrated her fiftieth birthday. Actually, it wasn't really a celebration as such—more of a 'thank God I've escaped that marriage'. Yes, another one. To be fair, she knew it was a fifty-fifty thing; she had to take some of the blame. Pure inability to let go and trust a man after him. She refused to use his name now. Taboo. Couldn't—refused to form the sounds that made up his name. Hadn't done so for twenty years. Now single again, she needed to step back and take time to review her life. She was relieved and delighted when her good friend Mave invited her to get away for a while and join her at her new home in Cirencester.

Absolute bliss, thought Katia as she arrived one Monday morning in the ancient town. She marvelled at the beauty of its golden stone; this place really was a hidden gem. She loved her home in London, but every now and then she would get overwhelmed by the queues and the restless heaving crowds. It felt so good to escape for a week or so. And chill.

Katia smiled broadly as she hugged Mave. 'It's just so great to see you. It's been too long …

But hey, you look amazing.'

'Thanks.' said Mave, 'Come and have a cuppa and then you can check out the town this afternoon while I finish a bloody report that's been demanding to be finished for days. I don't know... I'm constantly playing catch up these days. Tonight—I'm all yours.'

Katia felt quite restored as she sat outside a coffee shop. Her shades were on, her head thrown back as her face absorbed the warmth of the early autumn sun. She became aware that she was savouring the minutes. She was welcoming the present and maybe, just maybe, this could lead to a brighter future.

She spent most of the afternoon strolling along the central streets eyeing the feast of independent shops and getting a sense of the rich Roman history of the town. Eventually she stopped and entered a book-store; she left this to the last because she wanted to savour every moment. An hour or so of browsing was such a rare treat.

As she scanned the shelves, she raised her hand to reach for a book, but quickly withdrew it as she glanced to the right. She had no idea why she turned in that direction, but what she saw made her heart hammer and her legs unstable. Sheer panic dried her mouth as she stifled a small cry and fought to keep upright. Twenty years is a long time. Were her senses still alive to him? Oh my God, was it his smell? Yes it was. It was his aftershave. She inhaled deeply and in that moment she forgot to remember and was filled with the knowledge of him. But that was only a moment when her hatred of him was briefly suspended. The deep emotional bond of hatred was trapped in time.

She shifted to a more secure position where she could view him without fear of being seen. His back was now turned, but there was no mistaking the shape of his head, the oddly child-like small ears or his preferred stance of right shoulder set slightly higher than the left.

Or did it used to be the other way round? Less than five metres away stood the man who, twenty years ago, had disappeared without trace exactly one week before their wedding day.

She had wondered why he was so adamant about not buying but renting a home together. Lots of talk about needing to be sure the location was right, if the commute was doable. He'd known then hadn't he? … Hadn't the guts to…

That of course was the reason for his edginess. He was preparing for the big retreat wasn't he? What had happened to her sixth sense then? It should have been in-your-face obvious that he was backing out. She chided herself—what a fool. And then that Friday, fixed in time. She'd hurried from work—dizzy with excitement; seven days to go, still so much to do. Shaky fingers making several attempts to put the key in the lock. Finally it turned and she flew into the hall where she picked up a note bearing her name, flicked it open and stopped. Shopping-bag thudded, keys clattered, as they hit the tiled floor. She sank down at the bottom of the stairs, closed her eyes and clutched her knees as if wanting to shut out the present and halt the future she desperately didn't want to happen. Because she knew it would be without him.

Many minutes passed until she found the courage to face the here and now. The letter—no, the note—it was only a note, lay in her hands. All that remained of the man she loved was a 'Sorry but I guess I'm not the marrying kind', kind of note. And then that chilling P.S., 'And please—a clean break. Do not look for me.'

The humiliation had been monumental: so many 'I told you so' murmurings—except they didn't, nobody said a damn thing. So many mealy-mouthed, pitying sideways glances. But most of all it was the grief. The anger.

The bastard.

And now, camera like, she focused on him. Tall shelves filled with paperbacks and small tables displaying the latest hardbacks, swam into a bleary backdrop. Voices became distant and faces blank. Now he turned, book in hand, and settled on a low stool to read. Katia held her breath as he revealed a much worn face. Was it really him? Never had she been more aware of time, that master of stealth, that robber of youth. His receding hairline created a curve or slope that somehow lengthened his face. It always was quite long, but now took on a rather comical marrow-shape. And the marrow-shape was not at all enhanced by the presence of jowls. Definitely not a good look. Had he always jiggled a leg when concentrating? She couldn't remember that. Must be a new affliction.

She took care not to stare too long, but glanced occasionally at her book. His image began to change as the years slipped back. Slowly at first, then gathering speed, as if time and memory galloped as one, to arrive at his former youth. She allowed herself a fleeting focus. She saw the sweep of light brown hair and firm, square jawline. And yes, there was that seductive smile. So full of charm and promise. Oh how he would have hated the thinning and the greying of his hair, steadily creeping back. He would have fussed and fretted. He would have searched for useless remedies to hold back the insidious decay, the unforgiving product of time itself. And that toned body so strong and virile; where was it now? A bulky, loose figure remained. Had he given up? She wondered why. And what about that seductive smile? Of course she knew what lurked behind it: a cowardly weakness; a deserted promise. She wished she could warn people right here and now. Don't trust that smile, it's barren; it will harm you. Stay away. The bastard.

She remained where she was, but wondered if he would recognise her now. She had lost weight—quite a bit; the once apple-cheeks were now gone and replaced by a much slimmer, gaunt face lined by time. A face that was recently framed by darker, short hair fashioned into a bob. At least her newly acquired big specs were smart and extremely cool—well, so people said.

A sudden movement caused a small panic: he was leaving and moving towards the door. In those five seconds Katia knew exactly what to do. An epiphany of sorts. She would not call out his name; she would not run to grab his arm. This, she realised, could be the opportunity for revenge. She must remain unseen, but she would follow him. And so silently and sure-footedly, she too left the bookstore. She was oblivious to the cool rain that pricked, needle-like at cheeks and bare legs. She tracked his every move as he weaved his way through the early evening shoppers. But a fleeting question presented itself: what if he's heading for a car park? This fragile connection would all too soon be severed. She was on foot. But no. He continued his walk away from the centre of town as Katia followed him at a discreet distance on the opposite side of the road. Her hood sheltered her hair from the rain, and thankfully, shielded her identity.

Now he made a right turn into a quiet street, lined with terraced houses and neat front gardens. He strode quickly, his head bowed against the rain until he reached a pale blue front door. His front door? She slowed her pace then stood in a bus shelter, where she watched him reach into his pockets searching for a key? It didn't seem to be where he thought it would be. More checking of pockets before he stooped to search for something—a key she presumed— from beneath a plant pot. Within seconds he had unlocked the door, returned the key to its hiding place, and disappeared from view. The fragile connection severed.

She began to feel foolish, embarrassed by her stealth. But no, she needed to do this thing. She needed to know more about him. Did he live on his own? If not, with whom did he share his home? What was his routine? She would return. She would find out. She found strength in her resolve.

Retracing her steps to the town centre, she bought wine and savouries for Mave. Katia decided not to tell her friend about having seen him. This information was for herself alone. She would plot; she would scheme; she would action it— alone. Anyway, Mave would go ballistic! Wouldn't want to hear, wouldn't want to know. Wouldn't approve. But most of all, Katia just didn't want to waste precious catch-up time talking about him. And so, as she knocked on Mave's door, she formed the words 'Don't you dare mention him,' in her head.

'Hey, Mave, I've had a gorgeous afternoon... And here's wine and goodies for my lovely friend.'

'Oh, you shouldn't have... but thanks. Let's tuck in—no time like the present.' And as Mave moved into the living room she turned to look at Katia again. 'I have to say, you're looking kind of... I don't know... kind of frisky. What've you been up to?'

'Nothing really,' said Katia, 'just been enjoying your delightful town.'

'Well, you've certainly perked up. Good. Suits you.'

The two friends enjoyed an evening of food, wine and chat. At intervals, mere tittle- tattle, but essentially serious stuff; stuff that enraged and perplexed these middle-aged women and demanded answers. Katia's voice could be heard less and less: she just nodded or shook her head in agreement or disapproval as her thoughts lost focus and drifted away to attach themselves to the future. What she was compelled to do.

The cruel finality of that note, two decades ago, had sickened her, lacing her life year after year with slow, deliberate pain. Enough! This was the time; this surely was the opportunity. She would have him. Because she could, couldn't she? She held the ace, didn't she? The upper hand. She held the knowledge—he didn't. She just needed to discover a little more—then boom! She'd have him. OK, it was risky but so what... It was about time... And yeah, he's probably still carefree and happy—yeah definitely happy given that he stole her happiness to double up his own! Was she the only one he'd fucked over? Oh, the bastard!

She became agitated and knocked over her glass of wine; the deep red seeped into the plate of savouries, changing their colour and texture into a distinctly unsavoury mess. 'Ohh, no... I'm so sorry Mave ... I've ruined—'

'No, don't worry, really... It's nothing. I... I was beginning to wonder... You'd gone awfully quiet... Distracted even. You OK?'

'Yeah, I'm fine. Probably a bit knackered now... You know how you can suddenly flump after a high—'

'Absolutely. Bed now hey? I'll be in London tomorrow and Wednesday morning, but help yourself to whatever and make yourself at home. See you about two-ish.'

Katia's dreams led her to new and imagined silent places. They unfolded the years and laid bare his life. She saw the intervening years, in close-up. She saw again the beauty of his youth; his mouth moved, she saw the words, but could not hear them. Memory is time; they are inextricably linked. Her memory was dragged through the years. She saw him change, his youth plundered and stolen until little remained. Gone was the seductive smile, the irrepressible energy, the effortless charm. His mouth moved; she saw the words, but did not try to hear them. His chance had gone. She ignored his silent pleas. The ignoble sentiment.

A glorious sunrise welcomed a new day. Broad bands of tangerine and cerise lay upon a fine sliver of gold. It filled Katia's heart as she sat in her parked car a short distance from his pale blue front door. Good. She was relieved to find that hers was one of many cars parked in the terraced street. A lone car would be so conspicuous in a street full of curtain twitchers—but not here. Nothing moved, except a scrap of litter being blown, tumbling against its will, down the street. Minutes dragged their heels, refusing to move along at an acceptable pace, but she dared not read, lest she missed him—or someone else, as they left for work.

At seven o'clock, there he was, slamming the front door. His hand swept his head as he made long strides down the street, away from her. She watched him until he became a tiny figure—one you could fit into the palm of your hand. And crush.

She waited for a further two hours because it was worth it; she had to know. But there was no-one. No-one else left the house. She would be back the next day to be sure about his, and indeed any other occupant's, routine. This of course was no way to spend part of a holiday, but at least she had the rest of the day to pursue more relaxing—more enjoyable, activities. But she couldn't relax, couldn't loosen the grip; she was marching along with every beat of the day, wanting to cheat time, to make tomorrow come.

The following day found Katia repeating her watch. He was the only person she saw entering or leaving the house. She knew she ran the risk of being spotted, but it had to be done. Feeling quite confident about his routine, she decided to view the house from the back. She had discovered an alley that ran the length of the street, and so having counted the number of houses from the end, was able to identify his house. Alone in the alley, she paused to consider her actions: OK, what if ... No, no, it'll be fine... Can say I was looking for—something ... a ball ... a kite. I knocked but no-one...

She approached the back garden and nudged the gate—locked of course. But then she noticed one of the wide fence panels was loose, so she wriggled it free and just about managed to squeeze through. She was surprised at how calm she felt as she moved along the perimeter of the garden. There were plenty of trees and shrubs, so she didn't feel exposed. She neared the house and peered cautiously through the kitchen window: very functional and masculine, no sign of feminine frippery. She glided silently towards another window: this was obviously a through-room, running from front to back. No sign of children's toys. Soft furnishings, minimal. OK, I guess he's single, at least lives here on his own.

And then she froze. And ducked. Strains of '*Come on baby light my fire*,' drifted across from next door's garden, as the male voice continued to warble and wobble through the whole song, only to begin again several minutes later. Meanwhile Katia remained crouched behind a rosemary bush for the entirety. She dare not move. These minutes had given her the opportunity to consider the foolishness of being seen. Not a good idea. If her plan was to be successful, she must remain under the radar of no-one. She must defeat detection. Eventually, all went quiet, no movement. No mowing or planting or digging, and so she felt safe to creep back down the length of the garden and out through the fence, into the alley, remembering to wedge the panel back in place.

✦✦✦

The next morning she was ready. At nine o'clock she slipped out of her car, a long, fair wig fitted neatly over her own dark hair. Urged on by blind adrenalin, she stood face to face with the pale blue front door. She knelt, fingers searching beneath the plant pot: it was there—the key; her relief was audible. She worked quickly, despite the hammering of her heart and unsteady hand. Now she stood in the hallway ready to begin, but first she needed to check all the rooms—she didn't want any nasty surprises. Oh, and yes... She should check out the back door; a quick exit may be necessary. She found the kitchen. Ah, yes, a simple bolt which she slid back. Just in case.

Moving around the ground floor, she was aware of no lovingly framed photos, but a space full of hard, cold surfaces. Little in the way of comfort. That pleased her enormously.

But there were three paintings in the hallway: unsigned but quite Hopperesque in style and technique. OK, Katia wondered, are these his? He must have moved on from his obsession with Frida Kahlo. She removed her shoes because the stairs were carpetless and she needed to maintain silence. Her bare feet trod lightly as she made her way to the top, and she was thrilled at the thought of every step she took, his footprint was erased.

She stood in the doorway of the front bedroom. Spartan living most definitely. The grim, stark bathroom revealed one toothbrush. This was a relief, for she had no intention of causing misery to anyone else but him. The door to the back bedroom was closed, and so she paused a little before turning the knob. She stood in the doorway and was quite staggered by what she saw. At least twenty paintings—his paintings, surely, filled the room. Some were hung, others propped up against the wall or on easels. They were mostly oils and urban scenes; she remembered he was pretty good—but these were very fine indeed. Perfect! she thought. Just perfect. She drifted towards the window and stood preparing herself for the next move.

Now composed and ready, she moved downstairs to the kitchen, where she worked her hands into her gloves, found the cutlery drawer and, with care, selected a large knife with a serrated edge. Perfect. And with enormous satisfaction she gouged a large letter K into the work-surface. The living room was next. The preferred K made a deep gash in the sofa: bits of stuffing spewed out as the knife slashed its way through the fabric. Most satisfying. Now Katia ran back upstairs, eager to make her mark. Back in the 'studio', she took her knife—dazzling silver in a ray of sunshine— and with careful precision, slashed a perfect K across every single painting. Each K, bold and ruinous. Each K leaving a trail of destruction across every urban landscape. She felt an exquisite sense of relief. The weight of painful memory, the heavy mantle of time could surely now be released.

She felt victorious; she had achieved her objective. At some point that day she knew he would return home and … Shame she wouldn't see his face. On her way back to Mave's, Katia considered his reaction and the effectiveness of her actions. He'll be devastated won't he? Knock him for six—won't it?... The fruits of his passion, so cruelly destroyed. Yes! His callousness fully avenged. Yes! Hadn't he once said he'd love to be good enough to sell his paintings? Not fucking now he won't.

That afternoon Katia enjoyed a good ramble beside the river Churn and through Harebushes wood. Some leaves had begun to turn gold, others refusing to surrender their youthful green, had not. She felt enormously light; her head was clear and there was a tiny sparkle on the horizon. Was this what happiness felt like? Maybe it was; she didn't know. It had been so long... She'd give it a try though. She began to run back to Mave's, then slowed because her lungs weren't up to it—well, not yet they weren't, but they would be. Soon. Oh, she felt the ambition, the drive, the power to be...

At seven o'clock that evening, Katia was preparing dinner—a treat for her friend. 'Shoo, Mave. Go and chill... relax for a change. I'll shout when it's ready.'

'Oh thanks, Kat, I think I will ... I see you've bought a newspaper ... Never get to read them these days.'

At ten minutes past seven, Katia heard, 'Oh-my-God', ring out from the living room. Mave appeared in the kitchen doorway, newspaper in hand.

'It's him, Kat ... he's dead.'

'Whose dead?'

'Tony fuckface Morgan, that's who... Look, see for yourself, here's his picture—obviously older, but definitely him.'

She handed the newspaper to her friend. 'It can't be, because I saw…I saw…' The words slithered to a halt as her frenzied brain tried to focus on what she saw twenty centimetres in front of her. She fell against the door frame. The blur became still and she saw that it was him— Tony, the man who had abandoned her twenty years ago. And she read:

'Last Friday, the body of Tony Morgan, 51, was discovered on a beach in southern Spain. It is believed that he drowned whilst trying to save the life of a 9 year old boy…'

Katia stumbled into the living room, clutching the paper as she slumped into a chair. Her eyes as wild as her breath; her fingers clawing at her hair.

'Please no… No… How can it be?' She was sobbing now, 'What have I done… What have I… I thought it was him… I… I saw him in the book…'

'Now come on,' said Mave, 'you've lost me now. What're you talking about?... You're a funny one Kat. I actually thought you'd be rather pleased. The bastard's dead.'

Katia could only drop her head and moan, 'What have I done?' Mave knelt beside her friend whose face, now colourless, lifted and revealed eyes filled with panic and words so slow as if trailing after each other. 'I've done … I've done the most terrible… thing.'

'What you? Kat, you've never done a terrible thing in your entire life! Tell me what's happened?'

Katia recounted the day's events. At times she struggled to describe her actions, but then the words tumbled out in an unstoppable stream. Mave could only listen with growing disbelief. 'This is all too hideous,

Mave ... somehow I must make amends—face the consequences. But you know what, I've been so shocked by my own behaviour—shocked to the core ... It's rattled my caged existence so much that I think I've actually broken free from the pain of memory. Yeah, I think I've done it.'

The next morning Katia rose early. Her gaze was steady as she drank coffee and looked out onto the waking streets of Cirencester. Minutes later she climbed the steps of the local police station and approached the duty officer. 'Good morning. I'd like to report a crime.'

The Rain Simply Stopped

Ernest and Clifford Green were used to dust storms. For several years they had fought to keep the topsoil in place on their Kansas farmland; a land that had once produced golden crops with pride and glory, now struggling to survive the ravages of the Plains winds that whipped across the fields raising a rolling mass of dust clouds to the skies. Farmers watched helplessly as their crops blew away. The brothers, tall and lean, had seen scourging dust destroy their greening wheat. In response Ernest would clench his jaw, head held high and utter, 'I aim to try again.' Clifford would simply bunch his gnarled hands into the pockets of his sun- bleached overalls, drop his head and trudge heavily away into the distance. But nothing had prepared them for Black Sunday, April 14th 1935.

The day was warm and pleasant; a gentle breeze hummed and lingered out from the southwest. By mid-afternoon the Plains people had lost their day; an uncertain stillness clamped the region, the temperature dropped and chirruping birds began to chatter nervously. Suddenly a huge black cloud appeared on the horizon, then rolled in mercilessly, dust-laden and unforgiving. The sun was lost. No light could penetrate the dense gloom. Ernest and Clifford could only grope their way to their doorstep and wait. And wait.

The wind blew for twenty-seven days and nights. The brothers knew no day but endless blackened skies without light or hope. They learnt to live with the dust, to eat it, sleep with it, toil with it. Their hair went stiff and grey; they ground dust between their teeth, spat it out so it looked like tobacco juice, but it was just dirt. Ernest believed he could determine a storm's point of origin by the colour of the dust. Black was the very worst, and Kansas raised; it sandblasted your arms, blistered your face and entered closed eyes, rendering you sightless. Red hailed from Oklahoma and challenged the very strongest lungs, while the invasion from Colorado or New Mexico was grey with a heaviness that clung on, leach-like.

By the end of 1935 there had been no substantial rainfall for four years. Clifford packed his meagre belongings and headed out west; he was tired of his brother's dogged determination, tired of his useless hope and unfailing optimism. There was never so much as a backward glance; how could he bear the sight of his brother's abandoned face, his wordless pleading lips. Ernest stood on his ravaged land, tired eyes trailing after his brother for what seemed like hours until at last he found a voice and hollered to the wind, 'Why would I go someplace else? Everything I have is here. And it's gonna... It's gonna be better.'

But when the dreaded 'dust rollers' prepared for invasion, the sun would first become a reddish ball, as if to protect itself, then disappear. In turn, the sky would reluctantly, gradually turn grey. The air around would be deathly still and quiet until the dust would envelop you. At that moment you felt absolutely helpless.

To Ernest, a 'No Man's Land' existence became the norm. Every day he would scan the troubled skies, looking for signs of the rain that would save his farm from ruin. He tried to protect himself from the relentless dust by hanging wet sheets in front of doorways – but the dust permeated the tiniest cracks as it went about its destructive mission.

Rain was an event occurring only in dreams.

He believed the most breathtaking sight in all the world was mile upon mile of level land where the wheat, waist high, sways and hushes to the slightest breeze and is turning yellow under a flaming sun. Maybe tomorrow.

In his darkest hours, Ernest would turn his thoughts to Clifford. Where was he?

Was he homeless? Hungry? Restless to find work? He should have stayed; but he was not strong, Ernest knew that. Their father had preyed upon his weakness; whittling away at his very soul, refusing to believe that this soft, aimless creature could possibly be his son. The son who was expected to match Ernest in every way. But Ernest loved his brother—had always protected him.

Ernest hung on, surviving on cornbread, beans and milk that came from the one remaining cow which he kept in the shed. He used a harrow, just to turn the ground over so it wouldn't blow so hard. He borrowed money from the Federal Land bank and planted again, and again. Waiting for rain.

Finally in the Autumn of 1939 the skies opened. The day began much as any other. Ernest was planting seeds, head bowed, strong sinewy arms working the land. He felt a sudden shifting in the air; not the threatening rumble of the roller clouds but something lighter, cleaner. And then it came. At first the drops fell lightly as if they were unaccustomed to their use; then with every glorious second they multiplied and grew warm and strong until huge raindrops cascaded down upon Ernest's upturned face as he drank in the sweetest taste he'd ever known.

Blue Overcoat

Eddie nudged open his front room door and sighed. 'Jimmy man. Come on. It's nearly ten... Got the council coming... you need to make yourself scarce. Oh, and have you been round to The Shelter yet? It's just behind the market. They might help you out. Steve Poole's the manager. He's a really decent guy.'

'Oh, sorry mate... I keep forgetting. I'll check it out today.' Jimmy raked back his unruly hair and pulled on jeans that were a little short for his long, skinny legs. He knew he was pushing his luck. One month of kipping on a friend's sofa in a tiny flat was enough to test the strength of such a relationship. He had only meant to stay for a couple of days. It wasn't his fault; he was down on his luck—between jobs, you might say. He'd be alright at Eddie's place for another week or two. Or four. Eddie was such a good mate: the kind of guy who seemed incapable of using that very small word, 'no'.

Jimmy moved into the kitchen and searched for some bread to toast and a tea-bag. No tea-bags. You'd think Eddie would have... Ah, this would do. He caught sight of a discarded, used tea-bag in the corner of the sink, plunged it into a cup of boiling water and voila; breakfast for one.

Five minutes later, he put on his jaded brown jacket and slung an almost empty rucksack onto his shoulder, stepped outside and inhaled the brilliant blue morning.

A small pie, filling unknown, occupied his rucksack: it would keep him going until that evening, when maybe he'd checkout the Shelter; he'd heard you could get some decent grub there.

No, he wouldn't go down to the Job Centre. The initial assessment there had left him feeling like he'd committed a crime. A twitchy security guard had eyed him suspiciously—well that's what it felt like; and the 'adviser' spoke very slowly in measured tones as if he was daft. Jimmy had left feeling cheated and angry, certain that the grim atmosphere was deliberate. Anyway, they'd never given him a chance at his last job at the warehouse. Ok, he'd been late a few times but... And obviously he'd had to tell them a thing or two when they accused him of slacking— anyone would. He admitted to getting a bit 'hot-headed' at times. Not his fault though... his ma had always told him to stick up for himself. Nah, he'd go next week.

After skirting the chilly streets of town, he moved inwards to the market-place where he mingled with the shifting crowd, absorbing the buzz and friendly chatter. He watched the traders at work, their woolly hats pulled down over their ears to keep out the cold, their bodies wrapped in layers and scarves; and boots stamping the ground to keep toes warm. He watched the buyers, some pernickety, others falling for the sellers' charms. 'Come on my lovely, try this one... you'll look a treat.'

Lured by a need to find warmth, he made his way to the library which was housed in a massive Victorian building just behind the High Street. He sighed gratefully at the warm interior, grabbed a random book, and sat himself on a chair that offered him a panoramic view of the entire room. He liked to spend time watching all the visitors as they browsed, read and finally selected their chosen books. His eyes followed a fragile looking elderly woman whose hands trembled a little as she fingered her way along the shelves; indigo veins rippling on parchment white hands.

As he watched her, the memory of his Nan flooded back. He'd loved his Nan—crazy woman that she was. But yes, he'd known she'd always looked out for him—called him a daft bugger, didn't she? Then gave him a big sloppy kiss on the cheek. And yeah, she'd say 'Ere you are, here's a fiver. Now bugger off and get somethin' you fancy.' He'd cried at her funeral hadn't he? Big sobs … And angry, so angry. Why did she have to go and die?

A book fell to the floor. Jimmy leapt to his feet ' Hello, can I help you find what you're looking for?'

'Oh, no,' said the elderly woman, 'I'm quite alright, thank you. But you're very kind.'

'It's just that you remind me of my Nan...' He returned to his seat and continued to watch as people tapped on computers, searching the screens for facts and figures. Presently he would head for his favourite space, but now he was happy to do nothing.

Satisfied with wandering, his mind was ready for action. He soon claimed a position in the poetry section, where he stood, head angled, to view the shelves. A collection of Seamus Heaney's work caught his eye: he'd discovered him quite by chance—didn't think poetry was his scene. But yes, there was something about his words... what he had to say. He opened the book and turned to the first page and was instantly distracted by a small, pale blue ticket—the dry cleaning variety. Closer inspection revealed that it was for a man's overcoat and dated the previous week. His first thought was to hand it in to a librarian; his second thought was to... Could he? What about the time his mate Cass found the sheepskin – well tasty wasn't it? Finders keepers or what. A donkey jacket, that's what Dad was wearing wasn't he, the last time he saw him? The last time he saw him, yeah – called after him didn't he? He was only a little kid back then. Ran down the street after him. Ma stood crying, red hair flying... why did she ... he was mean to her. But the big black back never turned around ... never came back. Not once. He'd been such an idiot to even care about the sod.

Jimmy raised his head and glanced round the library, eyes fixed on a smartly dressed guy and thought... Just look at him over there ... Right smart he is. Bet he never feels cold on a winter's day. Everybody has a bloody right to be warm haven't they? Ma always banged on about rights didn't she? A lot of good demanding rights did her, though! What does it actually mean? But yes, he could probably get away with claiming the coat as his own— worth a try wasn't it? He was seriously low on clothes, so this ticket was a stroke of luck! Had to be. His eyes slid round the room as he slipped the ticket into his pocket. Had anyone been watching him? Nah, he thought not. He replaced the book on the shelf—Mr Heaney could wait another day, and made his way out onto the streets of Muttersby once more.

He patted the pocket where his new-found luck lay and let out a gleeful chuckle. Whose idea was it to demand payment in advance? He supposed that too many items of clothing were left unclaimed; a waste of dry-cleaning costs and bad, bad for business. But hey, what did he care; it just meant that his good fortune was growing by the minute. And he thought this was going to be another crap day! But what if he didn't like the coat or it didn't fit properly? Nah... didn't matter. What if they sus him? Well, he'd just leg it ... Remember that time when daft Dave got caught? He was such a crap runner. Not him though... What happened to that certificate? Bet Ma threw it away.

He entered the cleaners and joined the short queue. A slight unease caused him to shuffle a little. He approached the counter and presented his ticket to the assistant who promptly disappeared into the depths of row-upon-row of neatly hangered clothes. She appeared one minute later carrying a long, royal blue overcoat. Jimmy had never seen such a fine coat. He eyed the bright brass buttons and deep collar. He offered his thanks and hot-footed out of the door. He dumped the hanger and polythene cover into the nearest bin, pulled on the coat—a near perfect fit—and strode jauntily down the street. He felt like a million dollars in his royal blue attire, and couldn't help himself as he popped into M&S to find a mirror and admire himself. What a right dandy. What fun.

+ + +

He spent most of the afternoon parading around town and was momentarily taken aback when he overheard a passer-by saying, 'Thought that was Steve Poole for a minute... You know, the guy who manages The Shelter. He wears a coat just like that. You don't see many long blue coats do you?' Jimmy felt a nudge of conscience but then shrugged it away telling himself he bought the coat at a charity shop. So there. He stopped only briefly to find a bench and devour his pie. Except he discovered, to his disappointment, that the pie was old: the meaty contents were quite green and the pastry resembled some sort of cardboard substitute. Never mind, he'd go a bit early to The Shelter, where if luck was still on his side, he'd get a decent meal; he just needed to have a little chat with the manager.

A converted retail unit, The Shelter, was managed by Steve Poole, a reformed con-man. It catered for people who were down on their luck or temporarily homeless. Jimmy remembered to remove his overcoat before entering and stuffed it into his rucksack and walked in. 'Hi, I'm Jimmy. Have you got a minute? Sorry I can see you're busy. I'm looking for Steve Poole.'

'That would be me,' said Steve. They shook hands and Steve listened as Jimmy explained his predicament, 'My mate Eddie told me about this place. I'm jobless... homeless... but hopefully I'll be getting—'

'Ok, no worries. Finish putting out these chairs for me and I'll check in the kitchen—see if the food's ready.'

'Sure, leave it to me mate.' Jimmy whistled as he arranged the chairs and anticipated a good meal. Great. A delicious smell of curry wafted his way.

Steve returned from the kitchen. 'Everything under control. Actually Jimmy, you do look kinda hungry – come and eat now.'

Jimmy thanked Steve for the meal, promising to pop round the next day and help out in the kitchen. Feeling satisfied, he whistled his way through the doors, slipped into the blue overcoat and stepped out into the fading afternoon. One step. Two steps.

Parked in a side street opposite The Shelter, sat a motor-cyclist and passenger, clad in black to match the shiny flanks of the bike. Now the bike and riders were alert. A gun was cocked then fired. Once. Twice. Jimmy crashed to the pavement as a dark patch spread across the blue overcoat. His final thought being one of deep satisfaction. Such a lucky day.

Later that evening, in a fourth floor flat on the edge of town, two men sat watching the local news, eager to see the reaction to their accomplished mission. They didn't have to wait long. The screen was soon filled with the pavement outside The Shelter, scene of the murder of a young man that day. On the steps stood Steve Poole, looking grave and clearly shaken.

'Yeah, I just met Jimmy earlier today—seemed like a nice guy... About my age. I'd no idea he was in any kind of trouble...I can't imagine why anyone would want to... to kill him. And the weird thing was he was wearing a blue coat exactly like mine. The one that's still in the cleaners...Oh God... I don't suppose...'

The two men eyed each other in utter disbelief. One sprang from his chair, 'What the...

Billy told us that Steve Poole *always* wore a blue overcoat!'

Loose Innards

New York 1941

Roy held out his right hand. There it was, that tell-tale tremor. How he loathed it. He could lie; he could come up with a most convincing tale to fool the world. But that hand, the hand that revealed the ugly truth was beyond his control – damn it. He curled it into a ball and stuffed it into his pocket. There. He sighed, dropped his shoulders and checked his heart rate. Not bad – considering.

Outside, the street glowed pink and orange beneath the evening sky. His face grew bright with anticipation as he stepped onto the sidewalk, grinned at nobody in particular and made his way to the bus station. He knew he was way too early but that was OK. This time – yes – this time he had to get it right. No more chances. No pathetic excuses. No more apologies stumbling incoherently from wet lips. He caught sight of his reflection in a shop window. Not bad eh? He really had made an effort hadn't he? And didn't the new steel-grey hat make all the difference? He'd no idea what happened to his old one – absolutely no recollection.

As he approached the diner on the corner of West 25th and 114th Street he paused and checked his watch; still plenty of time for a coffee. And yes, it would be just a coffee. Not like the last time. The very thought of last time nagged at him and throbbed inside his chest.

He'd had a few shots of Rye to calm his nerves hadn't he? OK, he'd had more than a few, which made negotiating his way into his jacket quite tricky. But he'd be fine – running late – but Gregory would understand wouldn't he? He'd wait. Hadn't seen him for eighteen months now. But he'd been a fool to think that Gregory would 'understand'. What was there to understand? He couldn't even stand still – had to clutch Gregory's arm to steady himself.

And what had he said as he snatched his arm away? 'Your a waster. A loser and a waster. Sort yourself out.' Those words spat out – as sharp as tacks – penetrated his befuddled brain and chilled the blood in his veins.

But now the sky had drained of its beauty and had become a blue-grey mantle, darkening as he entered the diner. He called out a cheery 'Evening' as he sat down on the nearest bar stool. Nobody bothered with a reply. Across the bar sat a man with a beakish face and a cigarette hung from the corner of his mouth. But Roy's eye rested on the woman sitting next to him. Her red hair brightened the dullness of the diner and her dress of a similar hue was a perfect fit on her slender body. Were they together he wondered? Hard to tell. He ordered a coffee then felt for the newspaper in his pocket as he glanced at the clock on the wall. But he couldn't help himself; the opposite couple fascinated him. Their hands nearly touching; eyes nearly meeting; mouths nearly speaking. Roy reached back through time: it was his Rita – of course it was. The woman in red was her image. Of course he'd no right to call her 'his'

Rita – hadn't been for over twenty years now. But my goodness, he could almost feel those waves of red-gold hair that skimmed her shoulders.

Why had he walked away? Had he loved himself too much or not loved Rita enough? She'd made a mistake – just once – was full of remorse – brutal guilt had punished her. But pride, his damned pride had urged him to leave. To abandon her and his child. He'd wrestled with that stubborn, pig-headed pride for a year or two and finally hurled it aside. By then it was too late, far too late. She didn't want him back. Why hadn't he tried harder? Why would she want to reach out to him, the forlorn figure who wasn't big enough to trust her remorse and sincerity. He'd wandered in the wilderness for years.

He glanced again at the clock on the wall and wondered why time was in no hurry at all, just when you needed it to gather some speed! Back to the newspaper. Nothing caught his attention. The waiter washed cups; the coffee urn huffed out steam; and the clock ticked. Nobody spoke. The man with the beakish face inhaled deeply on his cigarette, his head thrown back and eyes closed as he released the smoke, sending its swirls towards the ceiling.

Roy had been making plans for a couple of weeks now. He just wanted to get back on track with Gregory... Needed to show him that he was a regular nice guy... Ok, there'd been one or two glitches... Well, he was human after all...And money really was very tight. He wished he hadn't lost fifty bucks on the game last night. He'd think of something. Of course he would. Maybe he could borrow... Hey, what about

Micky Malone? Micky owed him one. Yes, he'd give him a bell tonight. And if he gets slippery – well – he'd be forced to remind him that his good friend had rescued him from a very sticky situation a few months back. Gregory might lend him a few bucks for a couple of days – keep him going. He could explain the pay cheque coming his way sometime soon. Yes, Gregory would understand...

At that very moment he saw the clock. His brow furrowed as he snatched at his jacket sleeve to check the time on his watch. His heart thumped in disbelief. He jumped up from his stool as he called out, 'The clock.'

'Yeah, it's kinda slow,' said the waiter, 'Loose innards, I reckon.'

Roy's legs ate the ground as he raced along the street towards the bus station. He was twenty five minutes late. Damning words pounded his head. How had he managed to... What a fool...He'd promised... said he'd be early. I'll be there early, Greg – you'll see.

Roy slowed down as he neared the bus station. No, maybe he was wrong; surely Gregory would wait for him. He'd understand. Roy mopped his sweaty brow as he caught his breath and his chest hurt like hell. No matter, he was here now. He counted six people. And yes, there he was; there was Gregory, with his back to him. Couldn't mistake that stocky build and bright sandy hair. But it was not him. As the young man turned, Roy's face fell, and when it lifted he caught sight of the Philadelphia bus as it made its way out of the bus station. He cried out and waved his arms as he ran forward. There was Gregory, looking straight at him. No, through him. Face of stone. Roy cried out once more, but the bus swept away into the sea of traffic. He stood and stared into the distance; arms limp and eyes unseeing. Horns blared at him to move. Why should he care? He'd lost his son forever.

Dancing in the Dark

Patrick tried to ignore his cousin. Aged ten, Eddie was just two years younger than him; he was a pest—a large pest, not easily batted away. Or silenced. It was the voice that Patrick found particularly annoying: a monotonous whine in the style of a demented blue-bottle. And he was a snitch. Patrick had dropped out of Cubs because of Eddie who was the kind of kid who would even grass on his best friend. He would sidle up to the Scoutmaster in a low but familiar whine, 'Patrick's taken three and you said one. He has, I saw him.'

'OK, Eddie, I'll have a little word with Patrick.'

'And,' continued Eddie, 'And... Billy cheated. He never collected all those rocks, he got his big brother to—'

'OK, Eddie, shall we have a look at what *you've* collected?'

Of course Patrick could live with tale-telling, but Eddie was a bully and he loathed bullies—he needed to distance himself from them whenever possible.

He'd told his mother that some kids were scared of Eddie but she'd told him not to exaggerate, and anyway he was just a little boy and 'Be nice, he's your cousin. He's always got a big smile for me. Stop scowling Patrick.'

'Well *he's* not nice, Mum. He had a big smile on his face when he cut a black beetle in half...He actually cut it in half and made Lily and Annie Ford cry when he told them he'd cut up their hamsters. That's *cruel*,

106

Mum.' Mum wasn't listening. She began to sing as she whipped the egg whites.

One day his mother decided they would visit Auntie Mo's. Patrick was unimpressed.

'Be a sweetheart, Patrick,' said his Auntie Mo, 'and take our Eddie to the park. Here's some money for a choc-ice or something. No shortcuts by the river, mind... You know our Eddie can't swim.'

Patrick hated being called sweetheart—yuck! It made him wince and want to cover his ears. *And*, it was too bad that Eddie couldn't swim because he was definitely going to take the shortcut to the park.

Ten minutes later Patrick knew what was coming— could tell by the annoying jerk of Eddie's head when he was about to remind someone of his mother's instructions, as if Eddie himself *ever* followed his mother's instructions.

'Patrick, Patriiiick,' Eddie said in his usual whine that felt like a drill in Patrick's head, 'Mummy said you're not to go by the river. I'll—'

'I know, I know. But she's not going to find out is she?'

'Yeah she is. I'll...I'll tell her and she'll be mad with you,' said Eddie with a holier-than-thou face.

He wanted to knock Eddie into next week. His mother had threatened to do this to Patrick and although he wasn't entirely sure what she meant, it sounded quite painful. But instead he made himself as large as possible and glared at Eddie. This did the trick and Eddie raced ahead along the riverbank, then stopped and crouched down as something caught his attention.

Patrick held back, grateful for a minute or two of silence, but then grew curious to know what had caught Eddie's eye. As he approached his cousin he stopped dead. 'What! What are you doing you little shit? Eddie didn't move. A sadistic grin flooded his face. A dragonfly was trapped in his fist and he was plucking out its delicate transparent wings. Patrick, so incensed by Eddie's cruelty, punched him on his shoulder which sent his cousin tumbling and yelping into the river.

Patrick froze. He would never know why—for sure. He remained locked in position, fists balled by his side. As Eddie fought to keep his head up, the water fought to keep him down. His scream, so chilling, would be permanently etched in Patrick's memory. And then his cousin's eyes, so stricken with terror, were no more. The river had claimed him. The mutilated dragonfly lay on the riverbank.

Minutes later — he would never be sure how long — Patrick felt the tears streaming down his face and his thudding heart spoke of the hideous truth... And the consequences. What had he done? He saw his Aunt's face distorted in horror. Heard her howls... The disbelief. The blame. In a blind panic, he threw himself into the river but the current was too strong. It was too late anyway.

He climbed out; his lungs heaved for breath as he ran, dripping watery secrets all the way to his Aunt's home.

Patrick's voice rose in panic, 'I tried to save him, Auntie Mo. I tried. I really did… He ran off. I called him but I slipped on some mud and he ran off down the riverbank. I… I couldn't stop him and then he… then he…' His mother held her trembling child. Felt his trauma.

Patrick plunged his face into the cold water, and wiping himself dry stared into the mirror. Yeah, there they were, those familiar spikes of anxiety for all to see in his deep-set eyes. And his mouth, now restless, twitched and pursed—signs he knew only too well, for it was Little Eddie's birthday. Even after twenty years Patrick's mother insisted on a family gathering every year to celebrate Eddie's short life. He had to go, had to pretend, had to play their game, had to join in the absurd glorification of Little Eddie. Yeah, he had to go because if he didn't there'd be so much tut-tutting and cold-shouldering. He knew this because he'd tried it once. He could hear them now:

'Well, of all the weekends to take a holiday,' his Auntie Mo would say.

'Our Patrick can be *so* selfish… You'd think he never cared about Eddie…Pity he's not as thoughtful as us. He's always had a funny streak in him, you know.'

Yes, exactly what his mother would say to the assembled family. He'd go along with the bullshit, though— it was just a weekend anyway. Maybe he could get away early. He'd think of something.

And now, as he motored through the honey-coloured villages of the Cotswolds towards Monset, a veil of dread dropped over him—the heaviest and yet lightest thing he'd ever known. The beauty of the rolling agricultural land and secluded beech woodlands intensified his loathing for nature itself. He could trust the city: there was no betrayal there. Man-made in glass, concrete and steel, not the naked lure of the countryside with its unfaithful promise of tranquillity. Tranquillity my arse! Its secrets could kill; its beauty held danger.

He sat in his parked car preparing himself for the annual ritual: the coming together of his dysfunctional family, torn apart by the loss of its youngest. He was to blame for that wasn't he? He had no business being a free man—should be locked up; after all, he had 'murdered' Little Eddie—allowed him to die. Same difference really.

He knew the score only too well. He checked in the mirror. Yes, the tight grin was there. He was ready for his mother's measured hug, his father's little tap on the shoulder and uneasy hover. Then of course there were his older sisters, Connie and Clare, in cahoots as always, exchanging furtive glances. Did they blame him? Yes, they probably did, even though he'd explained how hard he'd tried to save Little Eddie.

His sisters were first to greet him. 'Hey, Patrick,' they said as they hugged him. He caught sight of his mother, and wearing that tight grin focused on a small patch of wall just past her left ear. Eye contact was too painful, too revealing. And there in the background was his Auntie Mo. No hug from her of course. Never had been since Eddie... A polite 'Hello Patrick. How are you?' was all he could expect. He found his father in the garden, as he knew he would. It was his favourite place; a place where he could inhabit another world. With hands in their pockets, they small-talked their way around the garden until thankfully his father took an urgent interest in staking the listing tomato plants.

'Actually, Mum,' said Patrick back in the house, 'I've got the beginnings of a bad head...Probably the driving... hold ups etc. I think I'll go for a walk before the meal. Maybe that'll do the trick.'

'Oh, well...' said his mother. 'If you must, but you've only just arrived... I would have thought you'd want to... OK then, off you go. Why don't you take your sisters?'

'No, Mum. If you don't mind...' And he was off down the path and away before his mother could find his sisters and make them join him.

He pulled his shoulders down and inhaled and exhaled deeply. Much better. He turned. There was the river: dark, deep and broad. Why was he there? He certainly hadn't set out to come this way. Hadn't come this way since... since... It was the lure of the guilty conscience wasn't it? It followed him around like a malevolent shadow—wouldn't leave him alone. Return to the scene of the crime and all that stuff. Was that what all this was about? Rubbing his nose in it... As if he hadn't suffered enough.

He stood still. He was three, maybe four metres away from *the* spot. Chest pounding, he didn't dare go nearer. Was it excitement or fear? Fear that the river might claim him too? No, that was irrational. He was a strong swimmer wasn't he. Divine intervention—that was it. No... No, he didn't believe in any of that nonsense. Anyway, he hadn't *deliberately* pushed Eddie into the water.

'Oh, *there* you are, Patrick,' said his mother as she busied herself in the kitchen. 'We were beginning to wonder where you were, weren't we Mo?'

'Why yes, we were,' said Mo as she strained the vegetables and spooned them into the best serving bowls. 'But you're here now. Go get a drink—dinner's almost ready. And here,' she said as she pushed a large tray in Patrick's hands, 'take the meat in.'

He moved into the dining room where a large oak table filled most of the room—took pride of place. The assorted chairs were very much the poor relation next to this handsome piece. Patrick sat down with his sisters and cousin Charlie, and so began the mock interest in each others' lives. Actually he quite liked Charlie who was a thoughtful, no-nonsense man who loathed small-talk, rather like his father. Come to think of it, Charlie didn't look too happy about being there either. Maybe he'd have a chat with him tomorrow—like-minded stuff, see what they could come up with to avoid next year's reunion. Maybe.

The family were all gathered now. A selection of meats surrounded by bowls of steaming vegetables, boats of gravy and bottles of wine—red and white—made a generous spread. 'Right, has everyone filled their glass?' said Patrick's mother, scanning the table. 'Let's raise a glass to Little Eddie.' Everyone held up a glass. Patrick wasn't hungry anymore. He gulped down the wine, draining the glass. He felt Connie's sharp elbow in his ribs.

'Steady on there, Patrick, you'll be pissed at that rate. You know it upsets mother.'

'Leave me Connie. Don't start. I can take care of myself.' He could feel the atmosphere thickening. Where was the air for God's sake? He got up and flung open a window, pausing to inhale the delicious breeze. He felt better and sat down, helping himself to a small portion of food.

'Eddie was such a sweetheart wasn't he, Mo? Remember that time he made you a necklace out of acorns? Made it at Cubs, didn't he?'

'Oh of course I do... I still have it. Means the world to me.'

Patrick wanted to throw up. Wanted to yell. *He didn't make it, he stole it. He was a thief as well as...* But he said nothing, just kept his head down and shoved food around his plate. Keep calm. Repeat the mantra.

'And he was clever wasn't he, Auntie Mo?' said Clare. 'Bet he'd be an accountant or something by now... What do you think, Patrick?' Patrick didn't think anything of the sort.

'I've no idea,' he said, turning to his sister and fixing on her ridiculous yellow earrings. Were they supposed to be parrots? he wondered. 'Maybe he'd be a politician—he was good at pulling the wool over everybody's eyes.'

'Oh, Patrick! That's not very nice. What do you mean?' said his mother whose nose was beginning to flush.

'Oh nothing—forget it. Doesn't matter.' He drained his third glass of wine and knew he should slow down. He was entering that I-don't-give-a-shit-what-I-say phase, but was beginning to enjoy it.

'Somebody bring the dessert and *please* finish the veg,' said Mo unbuttoning the top three buttons of her blouse and wafting her damp face with a napkin.

Patrick turned. His father was quietly working his way through the remaining green beans. Small neat mouthfuls, at odds with such a large man, he thought. He knew his father was safely tucked away in his own little world. Out of danger, out of blame. A quiet world where everyone was nice to each other. He wished he could join him.

'Oh no!' said his mother, jumping to her feet and searching the cupboard, 'I nearly forgot the photo... Found it the other day. It's a particularly nice one... Ah, here it is. There, see how adorable he was.'

Auntie Mo mopped her eyes and stood the photo on the table for all to see: a beaming ten year old—no, a grinning ten year old posed for the camera. Patrick knew what lay behind that grin. Eddie had been a cruel little shit and they'd all refused to see it... Or maybe they did. Maybe to recognise would be an admission of failure. Failure to raise a decent kid. So the next best thing was to *create* an image; an image of a child they had wished for: kind, thoughtful and strong.

Patrick threw up his hand and raised his voice. 'Bullshit! Fucking bullshit! And you know it... Every one of you.' The air was changed by a bolt of alarm. Cutlery clattered, sentences cut short. His father lowered his head.

'Patrick!' said his mother, her voice now thin with panic.'

'Shut up, mother. Just shut up. Listen to yourself.' He snatched the photograph, tore it in two and tossed it into a jug of water.

'Ooh! Oh Patrick... No...' said Auntie Mo, her face now blanched, her cry pathetic.

'You want to know the truth?' said Patrick, 'I'll tell you what *darling* Eddie was really like. He was a cruel bully. I'll tell you the real reason why I dropped out of Cubs—it was because of him. I'd seen enough of his bullying, his stealing, his tale-telling... Are you listening, Dad?' His father's head sank lower; his whole body shrank in a desperate bid to become invisible. Patrick continued, 'Remember Becky Barnes? Of course you do, mother.' He turned to his Aunt, 'You know exactly who I'm talking about, don't you? Lived on the far side of the park. I found her one day sitting in a heap, crying her fucking eyes out. Took me ages to find out why. *Eddie hurt me.* I asked her where. She lifted her dress and pointed. *He told me not to tell or he'd kill my cat.* I told you mother, didn't I? What was it you said? *Don't you dare say such terrible things Patrick. How could he, he's only ten. I'll not listen to another word.* That's the sort of kid your son was Mo. And that day... the day he drowned will haunt me forever. It's always there...the... the guilt. It sits tapping away on my shoulder, just in case I should ever... You see I didn't save Eddie that day because I couldn't. I froze. It was a terrible accident. I shoved him because he was torturing a dragonfly. He lost his footing and tumbled into the river. I couldn't move; my feet wouldn't budge and then... and then it was too late. I lied to you all. There were no heroics. I watched Eddie drown and could do nothing.'

There were tears and shouts of disbelief from around the table.

'How... How could you, Patrick? He was just a little boy.'

'You don't get it do you?' said Patrick as he shoved his chair out of the way. 'I've carried that lie, that guilt around with me for twenty years! Now it's your turn. Face the facts. It was a tragic death, but please... please don't go glorifying his life. And if... If only you'd listened to me—and to others—because Eddie needed help, maybe he'd still be alive today.'

Patrick headed for the front door, leaving behind a family blitzed by his confession, scarred by his words and stunned into silence.

He motored down the country lanes, feeling exhausted but euphoric. The release spread through his body and he felt a new lightness, a relaxing of those jangled nerves, those taught muscles. No more family reunions for him! He reached for his Springsteen CD and tuned into his favourite track, *Dancing in the Dark*—the one they were playing when he met Tasha, his girlfriend. He sang along loudly. He was heading home. Maybe he'd call in to see Tasha —nice surprise, she wouldn't be expecting him. Maybe pick up a Chinese on the way from his favourite take-away. Plenty of prawn crackers—she loved them. He was still singing when a front tyre burst causing him to swerve violently to avoid an oncoming van. His car smashed into the trunk of a giant ash tree. The music played on:

Even if we're just dancing in the dark
Even if we're just dancing in the dark
Hey baby!

No Harm Meant

Stay away from us. Roxy doesn't want to see you. You're dead to her. It's the price you have to pay. The last text from Rose, his ex-wife. He hadn't deleted it. The grim reminder lay in his phone; a reminder of the highest price paid for his single act of betrayal, witnessed by his fourteen year old daughter. That was eighteen months ago; he hadn't seen her since. But now he had a plan—if he could just speak to Rose first. If she would give him a chance.

The hot August day was stunning. The sun had burned through the clouds leaving a pure blue sky, startling in its nakedness. Frank parked his car and decided to walk the remaining mile or so to Lannacombe, to the home he once shared with Rose and Roxy. He strode down the valley. He knew this was a bit of a wild card, but if he could just catch sight of his daughter that would be a start. He couldn't believe that she hated him. It was Rose—he knew it. She'd got into Roxy's head—made her believe Rose was all she needed, the only one who cared. Well, that was a lie. God knows how many times he'd tried to call Roxy and written to her. Nothing. No response. In a way that was the worst thing. Even damning words would have been better than—nothing. But he got the message loud and clear, it boomed around in his head. You don't exist. If he could just be near her…

✦✦✦

When the house came into view Frank lost his nerve. He stopped and turned. Lured by the briny air, he clambered down into the bay and sat on the rocky shore. His hands felt the familiar warmth of the rocks. Memories of early fatherhood stirred his thoughts, his utter devotion to Roxy. His eyes grew watery as he saw her bobbing, golden curls and heard her excited chatter. Her hand, soft and trusting, would clutch his as they made their way across the rugged shore, stopping frequently as she gazed or squealed at the hugeness of the sea, or shrieked wildly at the sight of a great sea-bird on its way home. Her little fingers ending with nails like tiny shells of the palest pink. When at last she grew tired and the day had lost its charm, he'd lift her onto his shoulders.

A large sea-bird landed nearby on a rocky edge. A sea-eagle perhaps? Its brilliant white tail- feathers dazzled in contrast to the muted, warm colours of the rock. The water lashed and hurled itself at its spindly legs, but sharp-eyed and magnificent, it remained steadfast as its talons clung firm—waiting. Frank admired its resolve and its fearlessness.

He stood, swept back his wayward hair and retraced his steps towards the house. He clicked open the low wooden gate and paused to take a sweeping glance at the windows. No faces dodging from view, no sounds of activity. He tapped on the front door. He tapped again. He stepped back and lifted his head. He caught a blur of movement in a bedroom window. He was sure of that. He tapped again. He lifted the letter-box and there it was, that familiar scent of Rose. It was barely there but he knew it, that lemony, almondy smell that belonged to her alone. Or did Roxy have that same scent now?

He lifted his voice, 'Rose, it's Frank. I need to talk—just a few minutes, I promise that's all.'He wanted to add *I'm going nowhere until you let me in, hear me out. It's important.* But he suspected she'd call the police—wrong tack. 'Please Rose, just this once.' His heart leapt as he heard a chain being removed. Was he really about to see Rose... and his Roxy? A note through the door, yes... one that he hoped Roxy would find... hadn't seen them for so long and now... How could he prepare himself... in a few seconds? Had they really caught sight of him. He felt sure they had. So why... Maybe Rose still felt *something* for him. The door opened and there stood Rose whose upturned face grew hard as she locked eyes with Frank. 'What? Why are you here Frank? Roxy's not here. I thought I told you—'

The hardness of her face unbalanced him. He reached for the door-frame and his voice was breathy—urgent.

'Five minutes Rose, just give me five minutes. That's all I ask.'

She turned and walked into the kitchen saying, 'Make it quick... I have places to be. He followed her. It wasn't just her face, her shape had hardened—angular now. Had he done that he wondered. Yes he had. This was her defence against mankind. Trust no-one. They'll take you for a ride. He moved to a chair; the realisation—the emotion of it all, had weakened him. But Rose stopped him, 'No. Don't sit down. Say what you have to say. Roxy's away camping in Cornwall, so don't go thinking you can—'

'OK,' said Frank holding up a hand, ' I hear you. I want to know how I can make it better for Roxy—she needs her father—she's only fifteen for God's sake. And… and better for you… I'll do anything.'

She moved a step closer. 'This is the last time I'm going to say this. You crossed the line. You betrayed us. Roxy was just a kid… And nothing, *nothing* will stop me from protecting her from...from you.'

'Let me just see her—meet for coffee… anything. You can be there too… I wasn't well Rose when I… Everything was slipping away from me—including you.' He could see her colour rising, head thrusting, 'No. No. No. Go now Frank. Get out of my house'

He raised his arms to reach out to her. She flinched— why did she do that? She swerved to avoid his touch, then everything seemed to slow down but he couldn't save her; it was, in fact, over in a second. As she swerved she stepped back and skidded on a stupid cat's toy. She cried out and as she went down her temple caught the corner of the table. She lay still. She was dead. He knew it before he knelt down to check her pulse. In front of him lay the grey mouse. A fine spattering of blood on its rubbery coat. Rose's blood.

He sank back against a cupboard and slid to the floor. His head fell to his chest. He had never felt so alone. If he hadn't tapped on her door… she'd be alive now. She'd be behind the wheel of her car, on her way to wherever she had to go—some meeting, probably. It was a tragic, needless accident but who would believe him? And Roxy. His poor Roxy.

How was he going to tell her? He drew his jacket tight around him as if it might hold him together, and with the softest touch removed the pale green chiffon scarf from her neck and put it in his pocket. He had always thought it suited her.

When was it? When did it begin? When did she sow the seed of doubt? It had grown so slowly, imperceptibly so. She withdrew little by little—he hardly noticed. How could he have missed small silences that crept along but gathered strength and power. Why had he not missed her, you're-an-idiot-but-I-love-you, smile? He'd deliberately looked the other way hadn't he. For fear of... What?

Endless nights of wakefulness when sleep lay at the edge of his mind—refusing to enter, refusing to grant him a morsel of peace. He would plead for an hour; just one measly hour in which he could find longed-for release. As the new day dawned, his legs heavy with tiredness, would swing slowly out of bed; his head bowed and his eyes red. Rose would grunt and gather the duvet around her, to shut him out.

When did it all begin? Was it the slow creep of indecision? When he couldn't even choose a damned tie! Was the purple paisley better than the red? Or should he play safe and go for the navy. He didn't know... Precious minutes had been lost , he missed his train—the one that gave him a better chance of a seat. The day was already doomed and all because of his dithering, his inability to make a simple decision. Most days had begun this way, followed by the usual fumbling for answers to questions that weren't there any more. Faces turned to him as he struggled to find an idea; his palms now sweaty, the insomnia dulling his brain. He knew he had fallen from grace. He had been found wanting. He knew the signs—all that negative feedback. Knew he must lose the job that had been made for him. But it was devastating when it came: *Best for the company, Frank. Best for you. Take a break. Get restored.*

It was three weeks before he could tell Rose. The rehearsed words stood heavily in his mind. They lined up refusing to fall. They were unwittingly teased out by Rose as she picked up a shirt he'd let fall to the floor. 'I must say, your shirts don't stink of sweat so much these days.' And she added with a sneer, 'Are you on light duties or something?'

Then the words tumbled out. He didn't pause for a breath: 'I lost my job Rose. They let me go because I'm no use to them anymore. Profits are down. Apparently I've lost energy and commitment. I am so so sorry.'

The shirt slipped from her hand and lay on the floor—a small discarded heap. And in that moment he knew that he, too, was discarded. There was no other word to describe the way he felt. There would be no encouraging words, no sympathetic pact. Her face hardened and closed to him.

'When Frank?' Her words lay heavy in the air, 'How long have you known?'

'I... I don't... Two, maybe three weeks.'

'And two weeks ago you let me go ahead with the new kitchen plans,' she spat the words out now, 'and... and you knew... Why the hell didn't you *say* something?'

'I didn't want to disappoint you Rose... Thought I might—'

'You mean you hadn't the guts to own up to...to face facts. You're letting everybody down, Frank. I don't know where you are anymore... I don't know who you are any more. Get sorted and... and get a job! There's no way we can manage on my salary alone.' Rose left the room and he heard her running down the stairs and flinging open the back door. He walked over to the window. She sat down on the garden bench with her back to him, but he knew by the quiver of her shoulders that she was crying.

He knew he was out of his depth now in every which way. His anxiety had taken over—ruled his life. He refused medication—feared the numbness more than the pain itself. He withdrew from friends; he had little to say these days. Nothing of interest anyway. Eventually they backed off. You can only take so much negativity—he supposed.

He had no idea how he could regain Rose's trust—her love—her companionship. But his greatest fear was losing Roxy.

'Dad, you're not listening! Where's the letter about France? I have to return the permission slip today or else I won't be able to go. Have you signed it?' Roxy turned to her mother, 'Where's the letter Mum?' 'Go on Frank, tell her!'

'Roxy, I'm...I'm very sorry but we can't afford it... I've been trying to find another job but—'

'Oh Dad, that's so unfair! All my friends are going. *What* am I going to tell them? *My Dad hasn't got a job.* That is so humiliating. Dad... are you even listening to me? Dad... Dad, where are you going... I'm talking to you.'

'I said I'm sorry! What more can I say? He picked up his phone and jacket and made his way to yet another interview. But again his mind went blank. He had no ideas, no vision, nothing to contribute. His heart wasn't in it and he apologised for wasting their time and made his way home, eager to escape the noise of the crowded streets. Too many people with a purpose. He'd seen enough.

He saw little of Roxy. When she was home she was either in her room, 'Go away Dad, I've got homework to do,' or deep in conversation with her mother. The loneliest place, though, was in bed at night next to Rose. Her back always turned towards him now, seemed as solid as a wall between them. Could it ever be broken down? Would it be possible, with caution and great care to remove it brick by brick? He wasn't sure.

Walking was his new coping mechanism; fighting against inertia was his daily battle. He walked for miles to familiar and not so familiar places, and some days he would pause, take a break in one of the coastal coffee shops. One day he stopped at the *Coffee Bean* and sat in a quiet corner sipping his drink, absorbed in his thoughts when he heard, 'Excuse me, is it OK if I sit here, only all the other tables are taken?' Frank lifted his head. A young woman smiled down at him. She had a glorious smile that left him stumbling for words.

'Oh... Um... Why yes of course. I... I was just go—' He stood up quickly—too quickly, nudged the table and knocked over his half-finished coffee that dripped onto the young woman's sandaled feet. 'Oh, I'm so sorry,' said Frank as he bent down to mop her damp toes. ' That was so... clumsy of me. I...'

She put a hand on his shoulder. 'Please, it's OK, don't worry. And you don't have to go. By the way, I'm Tasha.'

Frank felt the warmth of her light touch. It was the kindest thing he'd known for a long time.

They met for coffee every other day for three weeks. Frank ignored the danger signs because he was beginning to feel he could recover. He'd lost that emptiness that weighed him down and was beginning to feel he had something to offer his family. One Monday morning Tasha said, 'I have to go to Budapest tomorrow.'

'Oh. I see,' said Frank, unable to conceal his disappointment, 'For... for how long?'

'Three months. It's a work thing.'

'Oh, well.'

'I'll miss our coffee breaks.'

'Me too,' said Frank as he tried to think of something to keep her at the table a little longer. 'I don't suppose... I don't suppose you could lend me your book of poems. I'd like to—'

'Yes, of course. It's just that I'm heading down to Gatwick this evening.'

'Oh, I see. It doesn't matter.' 'But I could drop it off at lunch time if that's OK. Where do you live? Unless, of course, you think that's risky.'

He knew it was risky but that didn't stop him from saying, 'It's fine. Nobody's in til late afternoon. We've only one car now, otherwise I would have...' He didn't dare look at the young woman now for fear of—something.

One hour later he heard Tasha's quick step on the path and he opened the door. She offered him the book, her smile was as glorious as before. 'Oh, that's great. I'll look forward to...' Their fingers touched. She took a step forward and their lips met. He broke free to guide her up the stairs. Nothing more was said.

The next words he heard were filled with tears and loathing as his daughter screamed, 'Dad! What... How could you...how could you.'

He lifted his head. The silence was enormous, as if the whole world had paused with baited breath, waiting for his next move. He saw again the body of his wife and seized by panic he struggled to his feet. Oh God, he had to tell Roxy... had to tell her it was an accident. She would need him now. Would anyone believe him though? They would know about the divorce proceedings and... and the gossip. Oh, the hell of it all! He'd never meant to harm her had he? But no, no, they'd say he hit her... In a fit of anger... Because that's what they did. My God he'd never, ever hit her. And... and Roxy would know that too...surely? If he could just calm down and *think*. Roxy first—phone Roxy. Tell her there's been a terrible accident... tell her to come home. No. No. Maybe the police first—they'd advise him about Roxy. And Rose's death... his fault... if he hadn't... Everything was his fault.

His hands shook as he reached for his phone and his words grew thick, filling his mouth. 'There's been an accident... My wife... I think ... I think she's dead.'

He fell to his knees and cradled Rose's bloodied head. He could do no more. They would be here soon. They would find his Roxy for him. And if he could make her understand that he meant no harm, no harm at all, then there'd be hope for tomorrow. And the next day.

An Important Matter

Bruce was held by a frisson of excitement as he entered his favourite room. Heavy metal sounds accompanied the beating of his heart as he closed the door behind him and inhaled the thrill that lay before him. His domain. His sanctuary. This was his 'becoming another' place, with its windowless walls of deepest purple and strategically placed tall mirrors. He stepped forward and ran his fingers lovingly along the rail of dresses, slacks, skirts and blouses — all with matching shoes and jackets. Money well spent, particularly in his line of business. He moved across the room to where his wigs sat obediently on their stands and stroked each one from palest corn to treacle-black.

It was Thursday, which meant he needed to be at his client's house by nine o'clock sharp. Mr Donald Wheatley, ex- governor of Stalling Prison, was a stickler for time. Bruce slipped out of his dressing gown and into his black and beige checked slacks, a cream short sleeved jumper and co-ordinating pumps. Next—and this was his favourite part of preparing for the day—came his make-up. *So aptly named.* His frame was smallish and so were his features. A blessing, you might say. And so, with a smooth, freshly shaved face he began his 'art' of concealing, blending and highlighting until he became Marie Bennet. Well almost. Marie always wore a short, light- brown wig of loose curls. Very feature softening. Ten minutes of voice training then Marie was good to go. She reached for a lightweight jacket, picked up her bag and stepped out into the morning sunshine.

As she climbed the steps up to Donald Wheatley's front door, Marie paused momentarily. And in that minute fraction of time she was overwhelmed by a desire to turn, to walk away. But no. The image of her brother filled her head and banished the worm of weakness. Not long now, Monday was but a few days away. She had planned meticulously. Two more steps and she was facing the front door where she used her elbow to press the bell. Then came the usual wait. *Come on, you know it's me. Damn you.* Eventually the door was opened by a tall and elderly man with a face as hard and angular as granite. Barely looking at Marie, he muttered something then disappeared into his study. A large grey cat appeared in the hallway to see who had arrived; it took one look then scooted off emitting a low hiss as it went. Marie could feel her body fill with fury as she wriggled her hands into rubber gloves and prepared for work.

She loathed this house. She loathed its frigid atmosphere and its walls that held unspeakable secrets. *I feel it, therefore I know it.* Such loathing boiled her blood as sweat broke free of her make-up and crept down her face until it came to rest in the collar of her jumper. She cleaned on, despite her discomfort and rage. But her heart wasn't in it. Why should it be? To Wheatley, she was a subspecies—a drudge. Her time would come though. It would come in a matter of days. The thought rallied Marie as she swept, polished and dusted. When all was done she reached for her jacket hanging in the hallway. And there, just a few inches above the coat hooks was the stag's head. *What an appalling practice. Wheatley's head would look good up there.* The thought sent a rigorous rumbling to her belly as she made her way to the front door.

Monday arrived. This day was anything but ordinary. Bruce had chosen the day: it was exactly five years since the death of his brother. Preparation was complete. The transformation began early but there was no need to shave today, absolutely no need. First came the thin layer of latex applied to his face up to the hairline. Once this was set, his usual make-up followed—subtle shading and contouring—nothing too obvious. When his wig was in place he chose a tan calf-length skirt and pale green linen blouse. *Well... there will be no cleaning today, so why not.* Marie was now ready to go. She stepped into her beige, heeled shoes, picked up her jacket and shoulder bag before setting off to the house of Donald Wheatley.

The usual wait. She pressed the doorbell again as she fought to curb the rising fury. *Cool it. Stay calm.* At last Wheatley snatched the door open, gave Marie a cursory glance before disappearing into his study. Not one word of acknowledgement or greeting of any sort. Marie stood in the hallway and took a long look at the stag's head, just out of reach. *Oh yes. Oh yes.* Her fingers flexed and relaxed inside her rubber gloves. She inhaled deeply, held and exhaled until she was still and focused. She remained like this for several minutes. *Come on. Go, Go, Go. You are ready.* And moving to the study door, she knocked sharply and entered. Wheatley spun round in his chair, 'How *dare* you. How dare you walk into my room—'

'Excuse me, Mr Wheatley, but I have a matter of great importance that I wish to speak to you about—'

'Well, Mavis, or whatever your name is, I have no wish to speak to you and don't *dare* interrupt me again. Get on with cleaning my house. It's what I pay you to do, damn it.'

Wheatley waved a dismissive arm at Marie then turned his back on her.

In a voice now his own, Bruce began, 'I wonder, do you remember me? You should remember me. Surely you remember my voice.' Wheatley froze; his fingers twitched as he grabbed the edge of his desk. Bruce took one step forward, 'You know my voice don't you, you heard it often enough. Five years ago my brother, Arthur Sands, took his own life in *your* prison. He was tormented and abused. I asked you time and time again to help him, but everyone turned a blind eye, and so did you —'

Wheatley screamed, 'Get out. Get out of my house—'

'Oh no, you won't get away with it this time. I've waited five long years for this day. Took a while to track you down. And as for the research and preparation— extensive. Turn round you cowardly bastard. *Now.*' Bruce spun the chair so that Wheatley was facing him. 'That's right, watch carefully. I wouldn't want you to miss a thing.' Bruce's smile hardened and fixed itself into a sneer so damning that even the room seemed robbed of oxygen and the day its innocence. His right hand crept to his head and removed the brown wig. His left hand reached for his forehead, where his fingers found the edge of the latex mask that he peeled away so slowly you would swear it wasn't moving. Bruce cherished every long second until 'Marie's face' fell to the floor, unrecognisable in a rubbery heap to reveal a face grizzled by a very short but perfectly trimmed black beard. Wheatley didn't move. His face rigid and his voice muted with fear.

Bruce took another step forward.

Exactly six minutes later, with his mask back in place and wig completing the 'Marie' look, Bruce hummed a triumphant tune as he made his way home. *Such an achievement. Such an important matter.*

The crumpled body of Donald Wheatley lay silenced forever.

The Replacement

The Grand hotel in Waverley-on-Sea had welcomed many entertainers to its stage in the Lincoln bar; but Roy and Ruby liked to think that they were the best. It was Friday night and the guests were ready with their G&T's, pints of pale lager and pretty pink cocktails. At precisely 7.30pm the pianist and singer swept onto the stage to a warm ripple of applause. Roy's black tuxedo suit was a little worn these days; sharp eyes would detect a thumb sized stain on the satin lapel and the trousers were baggily out-dated, but his shirt was as white as driven snow and pressed to perfection. Ruby, however, shimmered in a flawless emerald green gown and her corn-coloured hair took on a sunshine hue under the bright lights. She was in heaven. Tonight this was her stage— her time — her audience —and her Roy. There was no mistaking the adoring look, the adoring hand she let linger on his shoulder as he played the intro to 'My Guy'.

Ruby stepped towards the microphone, inhaled and sang those lyrics she knew so well with passion and pride. The audience was mostly men and women of a certain age, plus a handful of younger ones out for a bargain weekend where booze was cheap and grub cheerful. The applause, when it came, was warm — well-tempered. Ruby sang on as she swayed to the rhythm of the songs, but just as she reached the end of 'Diamonds are Forever' she felt a tiny catch in her throat and she reached out for the nearby glass of water. She coughed three times and threw Roy a fleeting, nervous smile but by the seventh number she was clearly struggling as the lyrics took on a strangled edge. But she held her head high, stretching her ample body as if to aid the notes now perilously out of reach.

Backstage, during the interval, Ruby snatched at tissues and dabbed at her thickly mascaraed lashes. Roy held her hand. 'Now don't fret, Ruby dear. I'll do the second set on my own. I'll be fine.'

'But it's never happened before. I've let them down. I've let the audience down… and they came to see *me*. Well I know they came to see both of us but…'

'Ruby, just listen—please. I bet your voice will be in fine fettle in a day or two. Honey and lemon all the way. Relax now and I'll take you home at the end of the set and before you know it I'll be knocking on your door at lunchtime tomorrow.'

Roy and Ruby lived in the same street—five doors apart. They shared a rather cosy arrangement. Now, an onlooker might think this was cosier for Roy— much cosier: he was married but madly in love with Ruby, who was widowed. And no, Roy couldn't possibly leave his wife; how on earth would she cope on her own at her age? Well, that's what he chose to tell Ruby. Nevertheless, at 1pm every single day Roy left his house calling, 'Bye sweetheart' and hummed his way to Ruby's front door, walking with exaggerated strides as if measuring his journey in metres. Apparently Roy's wife was very aware of this little arrangement but confident that he would eventually tire of that 'fancy- pants, mutton-dressed-as-what's- it, singer'—done it before.

Next day at 1pm Ruby hurried to answer the front door, pausing briefly to glance in the hall mirror to check the sleek outline of her hair. Perfect. She met Roy's broad smile that set his chins wobbling and his hands outstretched to embrace her. 'Ah, my Ruby. What a vision.' Ruby opened her mouth to call his name but the only sound to be heard was a tight rasp as dry as the husk of sun-baked wheat. She felt Roy's disappointment as his arms went loose and dropped to his side. 'Right. Action needed. Ruby, there's no way you can sing tonight. I'll get onto Lee, that agent mate of mine —see if he's got a singer on his books who could do tonight's gig. Is lunch ready, my pet? Indeed it is. Right. I'll phone him after our lunch and... dessert'.

Ruby remained unwell for three days. On day four she was much improved and was regaining her voice. Roy, as always, showed his concern, 'Well now we mustn't rush things, Ruby my love. Your heavenly voice needs more time—more time to recover.'

'Yes, but—'

'No buts, Ruby. Just listen to this. The audience likes Cindy. Yes, she's doing really well for us.' At that point Roy gazed away into the middle distance. Was that a tiny sparkle in his eye? Ruby wasn't sure, but there was no mistaking a sharp frisson of fear that shot through her. 'OK, but I'm coming along tonight. I'll sit in the audience. I just need to hear her sing,' said Ruby.

'Are you sure? Don't you need more rest?'

'Absolutely not. And that's final.'

The stage was set at the Imperial Hotel. At 7.30pm Roy took his seat at the piano and with usual flair played the intro to 'Don't Know Much'. And then there she was— Cindy, sashaying her way around the stage. She was young; she was good; the audience loved her. Ruby tensed in her seat as Roy's eyes shone with pleasure— and something else. What was it? She wasn't sure, but was even more determined to get back on stage with *her* Roy. The next day Roy blustered at Ruby's insistence on singing the following Thursday, 'Well…I'm not sure whether…Erm… but are you ready?'

'I am and I will.'

'Ok…Ok, but I want Cindy to be there and sing a couple of numbers in both sets and just in case your voice—'

'There's nothing wrong with my voice now.'

Ruby sat down with a sudden dawning. Perhaps it would be a very good idea to have Cindy sing a couple of numbers. Yes, and then of course she could keep an eye on her. And so she agreed to Roy's 'compromise'.

Thursday arrived. Ruby took great care in choosing the right dress. Roy had always admired her curves so she chose the sapphire blue one that sparkled as it snaked down her body. She curled and teased her hair into an eye-catching style and was delighted with what she saw in the full-length mirror. Take-another-look-why-don't-you, was exactly what she wanted.

She felt like a million dollars when she glided onto the stage; this was where she belonged. Her big, warm smile reached the audience and they greeted her with cheerful applause. And there, at the back, sat Cindy—mermaid-like in silvery-green; her hair a little waterfall of bright, coppery waves. Ruby felt a bolt of alarm. It was only a moment but strong enough to make her reach out for the piano to steady herself. But hey, she was a true performer and so she sang five of her favourite songs with gusto and panache.

Cindy was introduced to rapturous applause and as Roy played the intro to 'Suspicious Minds', she curled a hand around his neck. What was she doing? To *her* Roy. Ruby's heart banged away violently, her hands trembled, she was losing control.

'You know Cindy is really good for business,' explained Roy over lunch the next day, 'let's see how it goes for a few weeks. I think the two of you are a great draw for the crowd, *and* she's so pretty isn't she?' Ruby said nothing as she fought to quieten her raging thoughts. A sip of water quenched her dry mouth.

'Roy, am I pretty?'

'Well, you're... you're my Ruby.'

She sat very still. Her mind and body knew only coldness.

The following day Ruby arrived home from shopping and completing one important errand. Groceries were neatly placed in cupboards and fridge. Finally, she carried a brunette wig and tortoise-shell framed spectacles through to her bedroom where she laid them beneath two scarves in a shoe box and pushed it under her bed. She held out her hands in front of her, they were almost steady now. She had done the right thing hadn't she?

Five days later Roy knocked harder than usual on Ruby's front door. Before she could open it she heard a very agitated voice, 'The damnedest thing has happened Ruby—the damnedest thing. Let me sit down, I'm all of a lather.'

'Roy, my love, calm down. Whatever is the matter?'

'Bad news, Ruby. *Very* bad news. Oh... I hardly dare tell you,' said Roy as he dabbed at his damp brow with his tie, 'Well, as you know we've a gig at the Belmont Hotel tonight and... and Cindy has disappeared.' Ruby felt for the sink behind her and clutched its edge for fear of falling. She didn't recognise her own voice, when it came.

'Disappeared, what do you mean? How?'

'I mean she's disappeared. I've been trying to contact her for the past five days. I wanted to chat ... erm, chat about some new numbers. She doesn't answer her phone, there's just 'please leave a message' and all that crap. I know where she lives but nobody's seen her. She's done the dirty on us, Ruby. I'm telling you, she's... she's done the dirty on us.'Ruby steadied herself and stood tall as a soothing balm of realisation washed over her. She moved to the table and sat down opposite Roy. Her eyes grew dark but her lips smiled as she reached for his hand, 'Well, I guess it's just the two of us. Again.'

Trauma

A brushed kiss on the cheek woke Vivienne Crombie before her eyelids opened to meet the new day. 'Back on Thursday. Hope the appointment goes well. By the way, Avril's here already,' shouted her husband as he disappeared from view, down the stairs two at a time and out of the front door with a slam so sharp that the letter-box clattered with annoyance. But Vivienne had absolutely no idea who he was; she had no idea where she was or *who* she was for that matter.

For several minutes, maybe half an hour, she lay unmoving as her eyes flicked around the room desperately searching for recognition; but nothing, no shape, colour or fabric meant anything to her. Was this her home? She supposed it could be as she noted that a broad gold band encircled the ring finger on her left hand. Her thoughts shuffled back to when she heard the door slam shut — she knew that he must be her husband. He had said he would be back on Thursday and something about an appointment. And who exactly was Avril?

The distant droning of a vacuum cleaner prompted Vivienne into action; she was not alone in this house. Could this other person be Avril? Without hesitation or command her legs were flung out of bed. Her feet flew around the room in search of clothes but stopped abruptly when she came face to face with a full-length mirror which stood in the corner of the room. She stared at the image before her: eyes as dark as winter pools; face unlined save for a single crease on a high forehead. Late thirties she supposed. A sudden panic held her tight. Should she just slip silently away into the morning? But without a name there would be too many questions she couldn't possibly answer, too many disbelieving faces, too many raised eyebrows. No, she needed something; she would discover small clues within this house before she could face the world.

Dressing with speed and indifference she stepped cautiously down the stairs, her hand gripping the bannister — its solidness giving her the courage she needed right now.

'Morning Mrs Crombie.'

'Er, good morning, Avril,' came the hesitant reply.

At the bottom of the stairs stood a compact-looking woman with hair the colour of light tan shoe polish. 'Are you feeling any better now?' questioned Avril. 'They say it's a slow recovery — can't be rushed.'

'I — I'm a little better. Thank you, Avril.'

'Right, well, I'll be off now. See you next week.'

Avril handed the newspaper to Vivienne and was away. Again the door-knocker rattled at its punishment. 'Yes, fine,' trailed the reply, but Vivienne was far more interested in the newspaper — the top of the newspaper to be precise — for now she knew the date. It was 19th November and she could begin to piece together who she was. But what was wrong with her? Avril had spoken of a recovery that couldn't be rushed. She was in no pain, no visible scars, body parts moved with ease.

But she had the date, she just hoped a diary could be found which could surely reveal vital clues as to her identity.

A small leather-bound diary was found with apparent ease. But wasn't this an intrusion of privacy? It certainly felt like one as she fingered and turned the matt cream pages until common sense prevailed. How can you possibly intrude on your own life? Her hand twitched as she read the entry for November 19th: King George hospital, Neurology department 12.15. OK, she would go. So this is what he was referring to when he called out 'Hope the appointment goes well.' Today was Monday, therefore she had three days to discover her life before he returned on Thursday evening.

She would travel by bus — someone would know the route; she hoped it wasn't too far. After selecting a fairly sober greyish coat and matching handbag that contained more than enough cash, she was soon walking purposefully down the tree-lined avenue, making a mental note of the address as she went. Within a few minutes she came to a bustling main street where heavily laden buses slowed, stopped, emptied and refilled as a matter of course. Vivienne approached a stop and asked a waiting passenger for directions to King George hospital. 'You'll be needing two buses, love. A number 5a gets you to the Town Hall, then a 127 is a 20 minute ride to the hospital,' advised a knowing little man.

Later, as she approached the hospital which stood grey-faced, its size imposing, her footsteps once quite sure, now faltered. What if ... wailed her heart; but no, her hands formed little fists as she marched stoically forward as the doors slid open to greet her. *My name is*

Mrs Crombie. My name is Mrs Crombie, she howled inwardly. The elevated heat of the building made her body prickle with discomfort; she loosened her coat as she searched the signs — so many departments, clinics and centres; so many faces, some cheery and efficient, others stony and inert.

'Your full name and date of birth please,' said the receptionist. Tiny beads of sweat gathered conspiratorially on Vivienne's forehead. Several heads turned in her direction and waited, but there was no answer. *I do not know my first name, I do not know my date of birth*, screamed her head as she turned and fled, running until her lungs hurt and tears blinded her way. She stumbled onto a nearby bench and let the late Autumn coolness ease her anguished thoughts.

What's in a name? The whole world is in a name. You may possess the qualities to inspire a nation, heal bodies, compose music to lift hearts and minds, but without a name you are nobody.

An insignificant speck. You do not exist.

She stared unseeing into the middle distance until her jangled thoughts found focus. And when her clenched hands released their grip of the bench, she felt her racing heart slow to a steady beat and her breath came quietly. *Am I a Frieda or a Felicity? A Rosalind perhaps — or maybe Martha — yes, Martha fits me perfectly ... If I could choose, that would be the one. Martha Crombie.*

Later that November afternoon she returned to the house that she understood to be her home. Opulent furnishings in the Edwardian villa suggested wealth of some significance. There was no evidence of children: no discarded toys, no tiny shoes or cherished painting on the fridge door. A huge wave of relief flooded her mind — the thought of not recognising an adoring little face, was too much to bear. As night fell and she began to move from room to room gathering facts and small clues with which to build her character, the cloying yellowness of the lamps caused Vivienne to pause and stand very still. It occurred to her that she didn't like what she saw. No comfort could be had from the contents of this house, with its unforgivingly sleek nouveau riche furnishings and precocious atmosphere. She tossed aside priceless gems encased in fine gold; blood-red rubies burned brightly while cool sapphires glittered icily in their ring sockets. She flung open the doors of a wardrobe; had she really worn these clothes? Such garish colours. So much silk—didn't she hate silk? And then she caught sight of a black shoe-sized box. She removed the lid and lifted out a framed photograph of a wedding day — her wedding day. And there was her husband, beaming with head held high and left hand encircling her waist — tightly. But there was another photograph in the box. She didn't lift it out but stared at it, then sat back on the bedroom floor, her breath heavy and her head scrambling to piece together what had lain hidden — forbidden even, for so long.

In the picture her husband sat on a black horse. A horse. Vivienne's lips trembled as she whispered the word 'horse'. The realisation was overwhelming.

The images danced before her. Vincent's words — yes, that was her husband's name — rang loud and clear. He had been standing in the kitchen urging — no, coercing — her into going horse riding. And then he said, ' Be brave for once in your life,' didn't he? She had tried so hard to be brave and say no, but she just couldn't. It would be easier to do it — to please him, wouldn't it? And... And... that was it — he'd fastened her helmet. So why? The horse panicked — that was it. She was falling. The helmet slipped. Falling.

She removed the photos from their frames and, finding a black felt-tip pen, drew a large thick cross on both of them from corner to corner. She replaced the defaced images back inside their frames and positioned them on Vincent's pillow. *First steps on the road to freedom.*

The small hours crept by — mercilessly so. She enjoyed no rest. Through the bedroom window she peered at the slender new moon, its gentle light so welcome in a night of thick darkness. She knew exactly what to do.

Dawn was brushed with a sharp chill as Vivienne prepared to leave. Thank goodness that over the years she had managed to squirrel away a very tidy sum of money — how wise. She must have sensed that one day she would need her own funds. And the jewellery — she would take that, must be worth a fortune. Well ... it was a gift. It belonged to her. Didn't it?

She began to write a note to Vincent, and was profoundly aware of her level hand and the steady beat of her heart. No hesitation. She would contact him in time. She had recovered. There was no point in trying to find her.

She could almost inhale the scent of independence as she boarded the train to Edinburgh. This was her time. She would rent a flat and find a job. The job bit would take some time — she knew that; her skills had been unused for quite a few years. But hey, she relished the thought of the challenge. Here we go!

Vivienne soon became the girl about town and was loving every minute. She began temping — the best way to get the feel of teams and expectations. She made friends and gained enormous pleasure from furnishing her flat in her own style. Three months into her new life she invited her friends to join her in celebrating her birthday. She cooked Italian food — her favourite— and bought some very good Italian wine. She enjoyed her new friends, they were so easy and filled her flat with a warmth she had rarely known since childhood. Glancing in her hallway mirror, she couldn't help but notice the large sparkle in her eyes that enriched the deep brown and highlighted the curve of her smile. At 10 o'clock the doorbell rang. *Oh no! Somebody's rather late. Not a lot of food left. Didn't think I invited anybody else.* With glass in hand she opened the front door and let out a strangled Nooooo. The glass slipped out of her hand and blood-red wine spewed a livid mark on her white velvet trousers.

Vincent.

'Happy Birthday Vivienne.'

The Leaving

He was stuck. He didn't know what to do next, and so he turned round to look at Esther—his Esther—in the hope that she would instinctively know that he needed help. 'Get on with your work, Emre. Ask Miss if you can't figure it out,' said Esther without raising her head. And what a beautiful head it was, covered in dozens of tiny plaits, each one secured with a brightly coloured bead. Emre had always wanted to count them one by one, if only she'd let him cradle her head. But no, she'd never allow that. 'No, Emre.'

Esther was by far the most popular girl in the class. Well, an observer would say she was the most popular *child* in the class. She was smart, proud and fair. Her deep-brown eyes were all seeing, all knowing; they could slap you right down with one sharp, withering glare or soothe your woes when they smiled just for you. Emre made it his daily mission to stand next to her in line. Usually he never quite managed it because his large feet got tangled with the furniture, or he was too slow at 'tidy up' time, and if he didn't do it properly Miss would send him back. Then he'd have no chance. But yesterday he made it. Slyly tidying away before the end of lesson—his eye had been on the clock—and as soon as Esther made a move he was ready with one big stride and there he was, standing right behind her and inhaling the coconutty smell of her beautiful head.

Last week he'd given her a brand new purple pencil. His mother had bought it for him, but as soon as she put it in his pencil case he knew he must give it to Esther—well, it was her favourite colour—everybody knew that. 'Oh thanks, Emre. That's so cute of you.' Emre beamed broadly as a pink tinge flushed his face and his ears wriggled with delight. He'd do anything for Esther: he'd definitely fight for her and save her from harm. He'd race as fast as he could, he'd even leave a game of football to be at her side. Not that she ever really needed saving, she could handle anybody with her choice of cutting words or a thump in the solar plexus from the lightning thrust of her arm. Emre was convinced that 'Do not mess with me' was printed on her forehead, and everyone but him could see it. Now, would he steal for her? He wasn't sure about that. And he'd get in such trouble if anyone found out. He might even be dropped from the school football team! Could he ever risk that? Hmmm. Split loyalties there.

But then Emre became increasingly aware that there was a shift in the status quo, in the form of Casper. Now Casper hadn't been in the class for long. He was a smart boy full of charm and brilliant ideas—Miss Edwards loved that, of course—but what really unsettled Emre was that Casper and Esther were often exchanging smiles. Big 'I like you' smiles. And whenever this happened Emre sniffed noisily, then his breath made an even louder whooshing sound as it left his body. Most irritating, followed by 'Stop that, Emre.' From Esther of course. And then one day Casper became a very big problem; Emre thought the problem was as big and as wide as a mountain. It was lunchtime and Esther's turn to choose her side for football. Today it was seven-a-side and she had chosen five to be in her team, so Emre was poised to join her—she always chose him. His foot was raised and ready to run onto the pitch. But the name that rang out across the playground was not his but Casper's. Emre stood rooted to the spot. Disbelief, humiliation, even anger as all eyes were on him. Some kids giggled and someone called out, 'Shame, Emre.' But he'd show them; he'd show Casper, he'd show Esther just how much she'd miss having him on her team. Emre positioned himself in defence, *Casper won't get a ball past me — let him try.* But Esther and Casper up front made a perfect partnership which made Emre fizz inside. It was too much to bear and he tackled wildly, his right foot kicked the back of Casper's leg, he went down and his grazed knees left blood on the tarmac. Esther glared, 'I saw that, Emre. What's got into you? Say you're sorry.' Emre bit his lip and considered a *Why should I,* but he knew Esther's philosophy of 'fairness first'—and she'd never forgive him if he didn't—so he unclenched his jaw and threw a hushed 'Sorry Casper' as he ran back to his position. The most insincere apology he'd ever uttered. When the whistle blew at the end of lunchtime, Emre smirked as he stood in line with his class-mates. He knew what he should do. The cunning plan forming in his head restored his dignity, and he'd like to give Casper a bloody nose too.

At break-time the next morning, Emre did not perform his usual bumbled attempt to line up behind Esther; he needed to be the last in line. He bent down to re-adjust the velcro on his shoe, snatching Esther's pencil case as he did so, and as the rest of the class were now out of view, he had the perfect opportunity to place it at the back of Casper's tray. Job done. Emre's ears wriggled with pleasure. Now let's see what Esther—his Esther— thinks of Casper when he's found out, mused Emre. He'll probably cry fat tears all down his chunky, white face and protest his innocence, but Esther will have none of it. She definitely won't want a thief as a friend. *Now, I just might be able to help find the culprit. Well ... I did say I'd do anything for Esther, didn't I?*

'Miss Edwards, my pencil case is missing,' said Esther as she sat at her desk after break, 'I left it right here.' Emre didn't dare turn round to face her but looked straight ahead and clamped his lips together as he fought against the snigger threatening to erupt. Miss Edwards bristled because she was about to begin the lesson, 'Does anyone have any idea—'

'Look Miss, it's not in *my* tray,' interrupted Emre as he leapt to his feet to show everyone. Esther regarded him curiously, and from the depths of her brown eyes a glint of suspicion grew and grew. Several children took out their trays, but most did nothing, as they waited to see Esther's reaction. And then Casper— who probably wanted to do the right thing—placed his tray on the desktop, and there of course, right at the back was Esther's purple pencil case. Casper's face burned with disbelief, 'But Miss, I ... I never. I promise I never—'

'Ok, Casper,' said Miss Edwards, 'We'll talk about this at lunchtime.' Emre's breath made that whooshing sound as it left his body. He had been hoping for mega punishment and humiliation. 'Stop that, Emre,' snapped Esther from behind. Emre distinctly heard her whispering, 'I don't actually believe Casper would steal. No I don't.' But he hoped Casper would lose his place in the school football team for the rest of the term. Yeah, how cool would that be.

At lunchtime Emre searched the playground for Esther, and there she was, sitting on a patch of grass, the beads in her hair twinkling in the sun. At that moment she was the most beautiful girl he had ever seen. But the warm glow he felt was dashed away at the sight of Casper who ran up to Esther and shook his head and made pleading signs as he knelt down beside her. Esther didn't send him away. Emre's shoulders sagged. His master plan was in tatters and his heart thudded heavily right down to his belly. He just didn't understand. He didn't understand because Esther hated thieves, so why … Now he would have to think about cunning plan number two. Something so daring but certain to succeed. Yeah, he could already see Casper's downfall on the horizon. And maybe, if he tried his very best, he could plot the most cunning of all plans and get Casper excluded. Emre's ears wriggled in anticipation.

Two days later, as his plan was almost ready and only one or two minor details to be checked, he was aware of a change in Esther. She had lost her spark. Her gaze, once striking, was now forlorn as she played with the zipper on her pencil case; open and shut, open and shut. Maybe she's sick, thought Emre. But he never expected what was about to come. Never.

Towards the end of the afternoon Miss Edwards called, 'Listen up Year 6. Today we have to say goodbye to Esther,' Emre's heart drummed, 'We have to say goodbye to her because her family is leaving London. Esther, we wish you good luck and thank you for being in our class. We will miss you enormously.' Everyone clapped loudly, except Emre, who was too stunned to move his hands together. He turned his face to the wall as tears trickled down his cheeks.

Outside in the playground children filtered through the gates for the weekend. Emre lingered, never taking his eyes off Esther for he knew she was out of his life forever, but he could paint a perfect picture of her in his head; one that would always be with him, when he needed her. She crossed the playground and came to him. 'Emre, don't be bad. I'll be watching you, from somewhere.' And then she skipped away. He could still see those brightly coloured beads bobbing in the distance until she was gone. He sank to the ground as he hurled his football at the wall. It bounced high and sailed over into the park beyond. Casper, who had been watching and without hesitation, dropped his bag and disappeared to retrieve the ball. He offered it to Emre, 'Do you wanna go and play? I'll just go and tell my Mum.' Emre swept away a tear as he moved to snatch the ball, but heard *Don't be bad. I'll be watching you.*

Watching you.
Watching you.
Her words rang a cautionary tale.
He took a long look at Casper out of the corner of his eye.
'S'pose.'
'Yeah.'
'OK, let's go.'